PENGUIN

BURNING BRIGHT

Born in Salinas, California, in 1902, JOHN STEINBECK grew up in a fertile agricultural valley about twenty-five miles from the Pacific Coast—and both valley and coast would serve as settings for some of his best fiction. In 1919 he went to Stanford University, where he intermittently enrolled in literature and writing courses until he left in 1925 without taking a degree. During the next five years he supported himself as a laborer and journalist in New York City, all the time working on his first novel, *Cup of Gold* (1929). After marriage and a move to Pacific Grove, he published two California fictions, *The Pastures of Heaven* (1932) and *To a God Unknown* (1933), and worked on short stories later collected in *The Long Valley* (1938). Popular success and financial security came only with *Tortilla Flat* (1935), stories about Monterey's paisanos. A ceaseless experimenter throughout his career, Steinbeck changed courses regularly. Three powerful novels of the late 1930s focused on the California laboring class: *In Dubious Battle* (1936), *Of Mice and Men* (1937), and the book considered by many his finest, *The Grapes of Wrath* (1939). Early in the 1940s, Steinbeck became a filmmaker with *The Forgotten Village* (1941) and a serious student of marine biology with *Sea of Cortez* (1941). He devoted his services to the war, writing *Bombs Away* (1942) and the controversial play-novelette *The Moon Is Down* (1942). *Cannery Row* (1945), *The Wayward Bus* (1947), *The Pearl* (1947), *A Russian Journal* (1948), another experimental drama, *Burning Bright* (1950), and *The Log from the "Sea of Cortez"* (1951) preceded publication of the monumental *East of Eden* (1952), an ambitious saga of the Salinas Valley and his own family's history. The last decades of his life were spent in New York City and Sag Harbor with his third wife, with whom he traveled widely. Later books include *Sweet Thursday* (1954), *The Short Reign of Pippin IV: A Fabrication* (1957), *Once There Was a War* (1958), *The Winter of Our Discontent* (1961), *Travels with Charley in Search of America* (1962), *America and Americans* (1966), and the posthumously published *Journal of a Novel: The "East of Eden" Letters* (1969), *Viva Zapata!* (1975), *The Acts of King Arthur and His Noble Knights* (1976), and *Working Days: The Journals of "The Grapes of Wrath"* (1989). He died in 1968, having won a Nobel Prize in 1962.

The late JOHN DITSKY was a professor emeritus at the University of Windsor, Ontario, and a graduate of the University of Detroit and New York University. He published four books on John Steinbeck and served as an editor for three Steinbeck journals. He also published four volumes of poetry and a collection of drama criticism, and wrote well over one hundred chapters and articles on subjects in his field, especially John Steinbeck.

JOHN STEINBECK

Burning Bright

A PLAY IN STORY FORM

Introduction by
JOHN DITSKY

PENGUIN BOOKS

PENGUIN BOOKS

Published by the Penguin Group

Penguin Group (USA) Inc., 375 Hudson Street, New York, New York 10014, U.S.A.

Penguin Group (Canada), 90 Eglinton Avenue East, Suite 700, Toronto,

Ontario, Canada M4P 2Y3 (a division of Pearson Penguin Canada Inc.)

Penguin Books Ltd, 80 Strand, London WC2R 0RL, England

Penguin Ireland, 25 St Stephen's Green, Dublin 2, Ireland (a division of Penguin Books Ltd)

Penguin Group (Australia), 250 Camberwell Road, Camberwell,

Victoria 3124, Australia (a division of Pearson Australia Group Pty Ltd)

Penguin Books India Pvt Ltd, 11 Community Centre, Panchsheel Park, New Delhi – 110 017, India

Penguin Group (NZ), cnr Airborne and Rosedale Roads, Albany,

Auckland 1310, New Zealand (a division of Pearson New Zealand Ltd)

Penguin Books (South Africa) (Pty) Ltd, 24 Sturdee Avenue,

Rosebank, Johannesburg 2196, South Africa

Penguin Books Ltd, Registered Offices:
80 Strand, London WC2R 0RL, England

First published in the United States of America by The Viking Press, 1950
Published in Penguin Books 1979
This edition with an introduction by John Ditsky published in Penguin Books 2006

1 3 5 7 9 10 8 6 4 2

Copyright John Steinbeck, 1950
Copyright renewed Elaine Steinbeck, John Steinbeck IV and Thom Steinbeck, 1978
Introduction copyright © John Ditsky, 2006
All rights reserved

CAUTION: All rights in this work as a play, including stage production, motion picture, television, radio, public reading, and the rights to translation into foreign languages are strictly reserved. Inquiries should be addressed to McIntosh & Otis, Inc., 353 Lexington Avenue, New York, New York 10016. Amateur production rights are controlled exclusively by the Dramatists Play Service Inc., 440 Park Avenue South, New York, New York 10016, without whose permission in writing no performance of it may be given.

THE LIBRARY OF CONGRESS HAS CATALOGED THE HARDCOVER EDITION AS FOLLOWS:
Steinbeck, John, 1902–1968.
Burning bright.
I. Title.
PS3537.T3234B8 1986 813'.52 86-4018
ISBN 0 14 30.3944 X

Printed in the United States of America

To,
for,
and because of
Elaine

Tyger! Tyger! burning bright
In the forests of the night,
What immortal hand or eye
Could frame thy fearful symmetry?

—WILLIAM BLAKE

Contents

FOREWORD

Burning Bright is the third attempt I have made to work in this new form—the play-novelette. I don't know that anyone else has ever tried it before. Two of my previous books—*Of Mice and Men* and *The Moon Is Down*—essayed it. In a sense it is a mistake to call it a new form. Rather it is a combination of many old forms. It is a play that is easy to read or a short novel that can be played simply by lifting out the dialogue.

My reasons for wanting to write in this form are several and diverse. I find it difficult to read plays, and in this I do not find myself alone. The printed play is read almost exclusively by people closely associated with the theater, by students of the theater, and by the comparatively small group of readers who are passionately fond of the theater. The first reason for this form, then, is to provide a play that will be more widely read because it is presented as ordinary fiction, which is a more familiar medium.

The second reason for the creation of the play-novelette is that it augments the play for the actor, the director, and the producer, as well as the reader. The usual description of a character in a play—"Businessman, aged forty"—gives them very little to go on. It can be argued that with this terse description the burden of character portrayal must lie in the dialogue and in seeing the actor onstage. It can further be argued that terse description gives the director and the set designer greater leeway in exercising their own imagination in production.

Against these arguments it can be said, first, that it can do no harm for theatergoers or theater people to have the fullest sense of the intention of the writer; and, second, that director, actor, and set designer cannot be limited, and may even be helped, by a full knowledge of the details pertinent to the action. And for the many people who have not seen the play, and will never see it, this becomes an aid to which they are entitled.

It is generally accepted that writers of regular fiction do not care, or are not able, to submit themselves to the discipline of the theater. They do not wish to keep the action within the boundaries of the proscenium arch; they do not wish to limit themselves to curtains and to scenes projected by dialogue alone. The usual play, then, would seem to be highly confining—and so it is. There must be no entrance into the thoughts of a character unless those thoughts are clearly exposed in the dialogue. People cannot wander around geographically unless the writer has provided some physical technique for making such wanderings convincing onstage. The action must be close-built, and something must have happened to the characters when the curtain has been lowered on the final line. These working principles are applicable both to the regular play form and to the play-novelette. There is one further limitation. The piece must be short.

On the rewarding side of the picture lie the concentration and discipline of the theater and the impossibility of setting down any vaguenesses either intellectual or physical. You must be clear and concise. There can be no waste, no long discussion, no departure from a main theme, and little exposition. As in any good play, the action must be immediate, dynamic, and dramatic resolution must occur entirely through the characters themselves.

The difficulties of the technique are very great. The writer whose whole training has lain in the play is content to leave physical matters to his director or set designer and has not learned to use description as a fiction writer does. On the other hand, the fiction writer has been trained to let his description pick up his dialogue, and he tends to depart from the tight structure of the theater. If a writer is not accustomed to *seeing* his story before his eyes, his use of this form is not likely to be successful.

Despite its difficulty, the play-novelette is highly rewarding. It gives a play a wide chance of being read and a piece of fiction a chance of being played without the usual revision. I think it is a legitimate form and one that can stand a great deal of exploration.

JOHN STEINBECK

Introduction

John Steinbeck published his third and final play-novelette, *Burning Bright,* in fictional form in 1950; the play text, which does not differ hugely from the novella, followed it into print the following year, after the play's unsuccessful New York run in the 1950 season. Like its predecessors *Of Mice and Men* (1937) and *The Moon Is Down* (1942), *Burning Bright* conformed to its author's notion that a new literary form could usefully be considered, one in which a work of fiction could readily be converted into a stage vehicle, itself one in which chapter transitions served as endings and beginnings for scenes and acts.

So it was to be with *Burning Bright.* Moreover, Steinbeck was well aware of the need for drama to have purpose; and indeed, the play version, which received Steinbeck's special, hands-on attention during its preparatory period, is even sharper in its emphasis than the fictional one.

But the play's language was more of a problem on stage than it proved to be on the printed page. Steinbeck clearly wanted the language his four characters spoke to be an exalted, universal speech that transcended the temporary quotidian; and the problem with flesh-and-blood individuals speaking such language from the stage proved too much for the original audiences to bear with. Originally given the working title of "Everyman," Steinbeck's play (the author later claimed in a hurt tone in a defensive essay called "Critics, Critics Burning Bright"), was meant to employ language that would "lift the story to the parable expression of the morality plays." Doubtless, many confused audience members must have felt they were watching an amorality play if they were able to get past Steinbeck's dialogue at all, for the latter seems imitative of something older than the medieval *Everyman*—*Beowulf*, say—in its use of hyphenated combinations of words.

The play ran for thirteen performances.

I

It was conceived as a work of fiction meant for immediate and ready transfer to the stage, and Steinbeck initially considered entitling the play-novelette "In the Forests of the Night," but finally settled on *Burning Bright*—an allusion to the same source, William Blake's "Songs of Experience," specifically "The Tyger," which is itself a riposte to Blake's own "The Lamb" from the accompanying "Songs of Innocence," where meekness and mildness are aspects of Divine Creation worthy of awe. Blake had asked in "The Lamb,"

> Little Lamb, who made thee?
> Dost thou know who made thee?

—and identifies himself with the lamb:

> I a child, & thou a lamb,
> We are called by his name.

But the God of "Tyger" is beyond comprehension, leading Blake to ask, "Did he who made The Lamb make thee?" of the "Tyger." "The Tyger," on the other hand, offers what becomes proof of an oxymoronic Creation, namely, the coexistence of gentleness and ferocity in the same sphere of existence. Blake's first and last stanzas pose the conundrum memorably:

> Tyger! Tyger! burning bright
> In the forests of the night,
> What immortal hand or eye
> Dare frame thy fearful symmetry?

Of course, the opening stanza simply asks about possibility and potentiality, and uses the word "Could" in place of the final line's

"Dare." The second word raises the poem's ante of meaning, for the former one merely expresses astonishment of God's power; but the second reminds us of what the virtue once known as "Fear of the Lord" meant: it is Moses transfixed by the burning bush and learning that God being God, no human logic can encompass God's power—which will have its way regardless of our standards of propriety. Blake was throwing his hands up at reconciling an all-powerful Creator—interestingly named in a lowercase "he," with the gentle "Lamb," the traditional symbol for the sacrificed Christ. This comes down to an attempt to see the divinities of The "Old" and "New" Testaments, the epitome of power and mercy, with one another.

So that *Burning Bright* becomes an apter title than "In the Forests of the Night," since both its terms—"burning" and "bright"—are operative in the final play-novelette. Both images come together on the last page of both play and novella in a way familiar to readers of the rest of Steinbeck, for the notions of light and shining run through Steinbeck's work throughout all his lifetime's output.

In the play-novelette, Steinbeck re-creates himself as the character Joe Saul, who learns to accept a hard truth from his mentor Friend Ed, clearly modeled on Steinbeck's own marine-biologist friend Ed Ricketts. Ricketts's scientific and emotionless attitude towards life had always provided Steinbeck with a polarity of thinking that he tested out by including a Ricketts character—that is, one based on his beliefs—in nearly every work up to and including *Burning Bright*. But although Ricketts spoke of something called "breaking through," he would never have proposed such a scene of transfiguration as that which concludes *Burning Bright*, Steinbeck's own way of reconciling values in conflict; and it is perhaps an explanation of why the Ricketts character tends to disappear from the works he appears in before they come to an ending—the way the admired teachers in our lives tend to do.

2

Several decades before the publication of *Burning Bright*, the Swedish dramatist August Strindberg had created a play called *The Father*, the plot of which centered around a domestic situation that features a woman driving a man mad by suggesting that he is not the father of his child. In this day of DNA testing with results subsequently telecast, that may not seem as much of a problem as it once did; but elaborate precautions were once taken to ensure that at least persons of "worth" were monitored so that paternity and maternity were relatively assured. Strindberg's males evince paranoia on this theme, not to mention male chauvinism and flat-out misogyny.

Similarly, only a few years after *Burning Bright*'s publication and stage presentation, Tennessee Williams's greatly successful *Cat on a Hot Tin Roof* premiered on Broadway, and John Steinbeck attended a performance and commented on what he saw as the neurotic behavior of its principal characters. (What Williams thought of the personae of Steinbeck's play—if he even saw it—has apparently not been recorded.) But in Williams's drama, a strong woman—Maggie the Cat—brings her husband Brick to the point of incipient fatherhood by sheer force of will. *Burning Bright* stands at a thematic midpoint between the Strindberg and Williams plays. For in it, a strong woman, Mordeen—surely modeled on Gwyn—conceives a child by a man she has no romantic interest in, and who is as disposable as a condom as the play's harsh third act shows—but whose husband eventually comes to terms with what she has done by rationalizing it in the name of universal parenthood. Just as *The Grapes of Wrath* argued that under conditions of stress humankind can produce new definitions of family, *Burning Bright* suggests that it is no insult to one's manhood to accept a baby sired by another man as his own.

Such acceptance may not strike us as an ethical challenge, but the work's brusque disposal of the stand-in stud character, Victor, may seem just a tad inhumane—or inhuman. But Steinbeck consigns the deed to his Friend Ed, that is, Ed Ricketts, who could feed a cat at one moment and objectively, coldly, turn it into a specimen the next. Steinbeck needed this last interjection of a Ricketts character into his canon of works to show that in the great flow of things, subjective morality was a luxury our species cannot afford; but he did not assign that role to his own character, Joe Saul, whose own reaction to learning that his child-to-be is not his at all is one of abashed confusion. A Shakespeare—or an Arthur Miller—might have put a knife in his hand.

As with *East of Eden*, Steinbeck's second and final "big" work, biblical reminiscences abound. In both books, one cannot but think of Cain and Abel, Abraham, Isaac and Ishmael, Isaac and Esau, and Jacob—especially the latter; but the image that dominates all is that of the foster father Joseph (Joe Saul), Mary (Mordeen), and Christ (the child) in the play-novelette's final epiphany. This subject has hardly been touched upon by Steinbeck's critics, and doubtless it escaped the scant audiences for the play's first production, but it does touch upon Steinbeck's insistence that the play would prove difficult because it was "moral" in nature. Steinbeck's Western morality must have seemed odd to audiences and readers in 1950, given the facts of Friend Ed's cold-blooded murder of sperm donor Victor and Mordeen's equally cold-blooded acceptance of that same sperm as though it were that of her husband, Joe Saul. Yet it would indeed be a strange theatergoer or reader who did not feel a twinge of recognition at the simple theatrical architecture of the work's final scene, an asymmetrical triangle patent in any art museum—or church.

3

With a cast of only four—but one that included Howard Da Silva as Friend Ed, Barbara Bel Geddes as Mordeen, Kent Smith as Joe Saul, and Martin Brooks as Victor—and with a production underwritten by Rodgers and Hammerstein (then at the peak of their celebrity), and with direction by Guthrie McClintic and sets and lighting by Jo Mielziner and costumes by Aline Bernstein, the question remains: How could the play have been anything but a money-earning success? And why would *Burning Bright* eventually get as little critical and reader attention as Steinbeck's early attempt at writing a pot boiler romance novel, *Cup of Gold*? The answer, if there is one, can only lie with the writer himself, whether it be a matter of structure, theme, or language.

So far as structure goes, the work is—strictly speaking—a comedy with an exalted outcome, so that Aristotle's "unities" need not be applied—not that they ever bothered Shakespeare. The play occurs in the time it takes Mordeen to conceive and bear a child, a natural enough cycle in the life of any reader or audience member. But it also is staged in four distinct settings, which may have confused initial audiences unprepared for what they would routinely be forced to deal with a decade or two afterward. That is to say, Steinbeck has created a play that employs four different settings, one of them the neutral space of a hospital room. Steinbeck also distributed the plot and its four characters in the longer scenes that precede the short final chapter in settings—a circus, a farm, and a fishing boat—where they obviously remained the same "individuals" but also established the universality of his plotline, an essential to the writer.

A problem may lie with what transpires between act breaks or, more accurately, between the time zones of one act and another, i.e., offstage. Recent modern performance practice has been to allow for only one formal break between acts (two at most), a policy meant to avoid paying stage workers overtime, and that presents clear problems with respect to the text of *Burning Bright*. For instance, assuming that the first two acts are played in sequence without an intermission, thus leaving a shorter amount of material to be played out after the break, that still leaves Joe Saul's conversion to Friend Ed's notion of universal fatherhood to take place during mere moments of audience time, not only drastically but unexplainedly. Therefore the onlookers feel cheated of the moment of sudden insight that realigns the course of the play, for reasons never made clear to the audience. One has to take on faith Joe Saul's change of heart and mind in order to accept it on such short notice. A contemporary theater could easily accommodate Steinbeck's changes of locale, but Joe Saul's blinding vision on the road to Damascus is withheld from us, and that is a pity, for surely a little effort from the lighting and sound departments could supply a sense of what occurs between the first and second scenes of Act III.

4

It would be hard to quarrel with John Steinbeck about the theme of *Burning Bright*. The notion of universal fatherhood would have seemed to him a natural offshoot of the idea of a single Emersonian human family that Ma Joad expresses in *The Grapes of Wrath*. As much as one might suspect that his stance regarding fatherhood in

Burning Bright is merely wishful thinking, he does have the convenient figure of Friend Ed Ricketts onstage to do the dirty work—and present the theory. The murder of Joe Saul's assistant Victor is something else: the play conveniently puts it on the shoulders of Friend Ed, who disappears and thus leaves Joe Saul without that notch on his conscience; and Mordeen's bad thoughts about the implications of her behavior and her superstitious apprehensions about their aftermath are wiped away by a few reassuring words from Joe Saul—a happy ending that even Rodgers and Hammerstein would have struggled to justify in one of their musicals.

On the other hand, though many husbands have willingly given their consent to the adoption of a child or children not biologically their own, relatively few have cared to have their mates conceive and bear other men's babies without advance warning, and under circumstances that would normally appear to resemble flat-out adultery. Mordeen's stated reason for putting Victor in her husband's natural place, that is, to give him the child that will inherit his genes and his skills, is premised on Joe Saul's continued ignorance, and thus on her assumption that genes do not pass on skills anyway, and that therefore it is better to delude her husband into thinking that he has been a successful transmitter of DNA than leave him despairing in misery at his inability to perform his husbandly function. In this respect, Mordeen is a Darwinian evolutionist while Joe Saul is, initially at least, a Lamarckian one. (Jean-Baptiste Lamarck (1744–1829) was a naturalist whose evolutionary theories anticipated Darwin's—except for one major departure, or "heresy." Lamarck thought that acquired traits could be inherited—which would of course save everyone a great deal of schooling. Joe Saul seems to believe that family traits are in his blood, his genes.) It is the coolly scientific Friend Ed who apparently tips the scales in Darwin's favor in Joe Saul's mind; but again, the audience—or the reader—gets no chance to observe this crucial process. Again, offstage action (as the Greeks well knew) can work more powerfully on the readers'/audience's minds than what can be depicted onstage, but *Burning Bright* depends upon a shift of ideas, not on theatrical action best left unwitnessed.

Thus it can be argued that the conversion of Joe Saul is (or was) wishful thinking on Steinbeck's part, a way of dismissing an immediate

dilemma by changing its terms. If Joe Saul's change in thinking between the two scenes of Act III is, as suggested earlier, an allusion to
the conversion of Paul on the road to Damascus, then the Greek Jew
and Roman citizen Saul—on his way to persecute Jewish converts
to Christian beliefs—is also struck by the blinding light which is the
main theatrical feature of Act II, Scene 2, and in the process must
become a "Joe Paul"—a singular instance of a quasireligious conversion being brought about by the influence of scientific thinking.
Paul's unique contribution to early Christianity was to emphasize its
universality, thus the play-novelette's insistence at its conclusion that
all men are every child's father, and all children the offspring of
every man. If this supposition is true, then *Burning Bright* is another
sign that the later Steinbeck was relying more and more on the
New—and not simply the Old—Testament. But this thematic up-
heaval is a great deal to expect a theater audience, or even a reader at
home, to accommodate within a few moments of darkness, or a half
page of white space at the end of a chapter.

5

That leaves the core problem of the language Steinbeck invented to
express his "Everyman" play, a deliberately timeless or dateless inno-
vation in English speech that resembles nothing ever heard before
onstage, on the street, or in church or a tavern. If John Steinbeck
had long before stated that he never intended to write the same
book—that is, the same type of book—twice, then as he began
work on *Burning Bright* two-thirds of the way through his career he
must have reflected on the need for not only a new and unique way
of having his story told, but also—it being a new play-novelette—
creating a new way of speaking that would serve for a staged play as
well as a novella.

Yet Steinbeck's earliest readers seem—after a lapse of half a
century—to have exaggerated the extremes of the writer's usages.
Steinbeck biographer Jay Parini does quote a familiar joking com-
ment from a critic named L. A. G. Strong that asked "Have I, I
wonder, the admirer-right to tell Mr. Steinbeck that this trick has set
me screaming silently in my reader-loss?" This clearly refers to

Friend Ed's usage, "friend-right," but in fact there are very few of these archaic locutions to be found in *Burning Bright*; it is more accurate to say that the language is often formal, ceremonial, as might befit speech uttered at a royal court or a cathedral event. This seems to tally with Steinbeck's desire to ascribe a certain timelessness to the events in his work, and most certainly to point to Joe Saul's emphasis on his family's traditional occupations—acrobat, farmer, fisherman—as though they represented genetic gifts. His enlightenment—or catharsis, though it is not tragic (except, arguably, for the hapless and disposable Victor, a walking sperm bank in the days when such things had not yet been invented)—happens offstage, and Victor's death is merely the coldly scientific final stage of a laboratory procedure. No, in the end Steinbeck's language seems most artificial—as if, somehow borrowing from his beloved Arthurian tales as retold by Malory— when he has the crucial exchanges between his own presence in the novel and "Friend Ed."

The language problem with *Burning Bright*, then, comes down more fairly to a matter of what literary and literate audiences can tolerate or can be persuaded to enjoy. John Steinbeck clearly relied on the sophistication of Broadway audiences and his long-established national readership, and he realized in the end that he had done what Lennie in *The Grapes of Wrath* would have called "a bad thing," for what he got was, instead, condescension—or ignorance. Only a new production—or the novella's reprinting—will ever show whether Steinbeck's experiment will, in the end, achieve a kind of timelessness.

6

Burning Bright depends in the end on a plotline which describes a process of masculine thinking—and attendant fears—that has to do with the question of whether one's personal sperm represents unique contributions to the presumably forward progress of humanity or can be—no real harm being done—replaced by almost anyone else's. Note that the work was written only five years after the end of World War II, with Nazi experiments in eugenics fresh in the minds of his audience. Steinbeck's notion at least smacks of a divorce between emotion and conception, a problem that is troubling still more than half a century later. As so often happens with startlingly new productions, *Burning Bright* may still be remembered—if at all by its initial and small audience—for its seemingly outrageous moments and not for its underlying moral lesson, which may have blinded even its author to its possible extremes of interpretation. The era in which *Burning Bright* was created was one heady with the promise of the United Nations; Steinbeck's message seems a global inflation of what has more recently been stated as "It takes a village to raise a child." His version is that it takes all men to be a child's father, and that all children can claim any and every man as their father.

We first encounter Joe Saul in the initial act, which has a circus setting. In fact, he is first seen in his dressing room, putting "dark hair dye" into his graying head of hair. There is nothing surprising about a performer using one or another form of makeup, but Joe Saul has a conscious purpose in mind: to disguise the aging process which he has already identified with his inability to perform his "family" duty to procreate and thus carry on the family skills, which Joe Saul dates back to ancient times. Victor, the eventual surrogate father of Mordeen's (and, finally, Joe Saul's) child, is mentioned with a kind of weary caution as an outsider who has taken the role once played by the late Cousin Will, who "missed the net" eight months earlier. Joe Saul says that Victor is "all right," but that "His blood is not my blood. He has no ancestry in it."

Steinbeck had earlier described, to a Russian audience, the status of writers in America as being not like the revered place assigned to writers in other countries, but as falling at a level "between acrobats and seals." In this respect, it is both odd and interesting that Steinbeck begins *Burning Bright* in a circus setting, in that Joe Saul is a high-flying, death-defying trapeze artist. The level that Steinbeck meant to be said as lying between acrobats and animal acts is the human floor of the circus arena, where the big-cat tamers and the ringmasters operate on a layer of sawdust. Steinbeck surely didn't mean that writers in America are ringmasters, much as he might have felt that authors can make something happen after all. Curiously, though Joe Saul is an acrobat, the presumably highest level of performer, Friend Ed is a clown, earthbound and just as surely tied to an idea of reality that Steinbeck must have used to epitomize his old friend Ricketts; and yet the idea persists that the clown figure in America is the writer, the person who watches the acrobats in society from far below. If there is a "seal" in the trio of male characters in *Burning Bright*, then surely it is the bloodless acrobat Victor, the id in this Freudian set of males.

Steinbeck had recently dedicated one of his more recent novels, *The Wayward Bus*, to his second wife. He also appended an epigraph from "Everyman," which had clearly not faded from his mind when he wrote *Burning Bright*, itself dedicated "To, for, and because of Elaine." The epigraph to *The Wayward Bus* could almost be applied to *Burning Bright*:

> I pray you all gyve audience,
> And here this matter with reverence,
> By fygure a morall playe:
> The somonynge of Everyman called it is,
> That our lyves and endynge shewes
> How transystory we be all daye.

It is because we are "transystory" "all daye," that is, all of our brief lives, that we are worried about progeny; John Steinbeck in *The Wayward Bus* was simply being intuitive—or prophetic. For it is in *Burning Bright* that Steinbeck confronts the issue of paternity in a crucial passage from Act I. When Joe Saul leaves Friend Ed with the impression that he feels cursed, the clown answers, in Arthurian tones, "It's time we sing this trouble out into the air and light. Else it will grow with poisoned fingers like a cancer in your mind. Rip off the cover. Let it out! Maybe you're not alone in your secret cave."

This passage refers to both the third act yet to come but also to a favorite theme of Steinbeck's, the idea of a man hiding in a cave-like place to figure things out— or to metamorphose—and then return changed but ready to do his duty as he has come to see it. This trope or motif runs from *The Grapes of Wrath* to Steinbeck's final fiction, *The Winter of Our Discontent*; but it also suggests an insecure and very private personality that can wear makeup to appear in public but also shuns publicity. Joe Saul's reply to Friend Ed is revealing:

"I know!" Joe Saul said quietly. "I guess I'm getting that way—digging like a mole into my own darkness. Of course, Friend Ed, I know it is a thing that can happen to anyone in any place and time—a farmer or sailor, or a lineless, faceless Everyone! I know this—and maybe all of these have the secret locked up in loneliness."

At this moment, Joe Saul guesses at what he does not yet "know," for he simultaneously predicts the progress of the play-novelette, yet manages to tally with the Everyman motif he has so far rejected. For now, Joe Saul wants to be neither "lineless" nor "faceless"; yet at the work's ending, he becomes both—even if, at the finale, he recovers his "face" in the act of renouncing his right to a "line."

Even in these quotations the reader can sense the stiffness of some of Steinbeck's language, which its author found fitting but which its initial audiences found ludicrous. Steinbeck's first major biographer, Jackson J. Benson, quotes Steinbeck in a most perceptive and prescient frame of mind:

> . . . to the average audience the whole subject of sex is funny if the audience is permitted to find it so. Sentences which had seemed clean were dirty to an audience although on test same sentences were clean to an individual. . . . The group mind of an audience is very different from the minds of the individuals who compose the audience.

The last line is tremendously revealing in the context of Steinbeck's career, or what was left to come of it. The "group man" was a concept he and Ed Ricketts had tossed around in the 1930s, and Steinbeck had tested it in works such as *Tortilla Flat*, *In Dubious Battle*, and especially *The Grapes of Wrath*. But as noted earlier, the notion ran into trouble during World War II, when in writing *The Moon Is Down* Steinbeck had to resort to an uneasy distinction between men in groups and men in herds to account for the disparities between a patriotic resistance spontaneously generated among an occupied people and the unified mind-set of the occupiers themselves. *Burning Bright* was pretty much the last gasp of Ed Ricketts's philosophy to appear in Steinbeck's writing—and just a couple of years after Ricketts's own death. Friend Ed being so clearly and closely modeled on Ricketts, it is hard to decide whether his appearance on his final outing is a last hurrah or a final dismissal. But of course, he is resurrected in *The Log from the "Sea of Cortez,"* published in the same year as the play version of *Burning Bright* and which is also a kind of eulogy for Steinbeck's old friend. And there is also *Sweet Thursday*, published in 1954, and which became one of Rodgers and Hammerstein's least successful musicals. The period of *Burning Bright*'s creation is, so far as Ed Ricketts is concerned, a kind of burial at sea for the marine biologist—abrupt, necessary, and beyond question.

7

Afterward, in the satiric *The Short Reign of Pippin IV*; in the semi-autobiographical "big" novel dedicated to his sons Thom and John (who never could agree on which of them was Cal and which Aron in that saga based on the story of Cain and Abel in Genesis), *East of Eden*; and in his final fiction published within his lifetime, *The Winter of Our Discontent*—as well as in his increasingly frequent nonfiction magazine contributions—John Steinbeck emphasized the importance of the individual rather than that of the group, which he even characterized as never contributing anything of importance to the advance of humankind. In this respect, the commercial failure of *Burning Bright* may have played a central role, if by no means necessarily a negative one. But by this time, self-effacement had ceased to be a means of sublimating the ego for Steinbeck, and more accurately a way of evading responsibility.

Just as Joe Saul begins the play showing concern about getting old—and therefore about the implications of aging so far as procreation is concerned—he is worried that his lack of progeny might reduce him to the status of a "lineless, faceless Everyone." Therefore, he effectively fears the light, which might reveal his anonymity or his ordinariness to the watching crowd below his trapeze. Less theatrically effective are the next acts, in which his fears are without real audience—though his discovery of his own sterility in his doctor's microscope carries forward the theme of the fear that his personal lack of distinction will be disclosed to the light of day. This reliance on the image of light, blinding light or transfiguring light, runs through Steinbeck's novels from the first decade of his career right

up to *The Winter of Our Discontent*. And it is in returning to the theatrically powerful notion of light that Steinbeck's play comes to a
close and "works" as well as it can.

Interestingly, the circus scene (Act I) takes fewer than twenty
pages in the play version; the second (the farm) under eighteen; the
third (the sea) under ten; and the brief hospital room finale under
two. The differences seem less drastic in the novel, of course; and it
is only fair to note that the scene and opening-action descriptions
naturally take up even more space in the play text, whereas in the
novel they become a natural part of the whole work of fiction.

But the novella's proportions differ radically from the play's. The
prose text's pagination runs: fifty, fifty-nine, twenty-seven, and
seven. Clearly, and unsurprisingly, Steinbeck felt more at home on
the farm, at least when not writing for Broadway. Performing the
play presents obvious problems inherent in the numbers cited; even
if a director in the present century might follow her instincts and
have minimal sets designed—and even if the hospital finale was then
more simply staged (as Steinbeck suggests in both versions), relying
mainly on a hospital bed, overhead specific lighting, and the two
(now three) remaining characters—just about all that is visible in the
play-novelette's world, the play is problematical at best. A stage with
a revolving turntable could help remedy the multiple-set problem as
well, but then where do you break the play? Act breaks might prove
too many for a play not all that long in the first place, while com-
bining Acts I and II with a single break and doing Act III's scenes
together comes to mind as a possibility, but that means pitting
thirty-eight pages of play text against twelve—and does nothing to
solve the problem of Joe Saul's abrupt offstage conversion between
the final scenes (as already mentioned).

Fortunately, the reader of the text presented here encounters no
such problems, though even if we are told *that* Joe Saul has changed
his mind we are never quite sure *why*. A sedated Mordeen, delirious,
is confusingly reassured by a surgical-masked Joe Saul that the dead
Victor is "here and alive, always." Now she decides that she is talking to Friend Ed *about* Joe Saul, who tells her that the baby has *her*
mouth, as if doubly accepting his (Joseph's) foster-fathership. The
reader must decide whether Joe Saul's homiletic explanation of why
he "converted" is dramatically or novelistically plausible, but it does

go on until the exhausted Mordeen finally understands that her husband has come to "know."

Joe Sauls's reply is a recital of what he has learned in his secret cave:

> "I had to walk into the black to know—to know that every man is father to all children and every child must have all men as father. This is not a piece of private property, registered and fenced and separated. Mordeen! This is *the Child*."

The appropriateness of this universalizing of an infant his mother has just been delivered of is for the reader to judge, but Mordeen ignores it, complaining of the dark and asking for the light. Joe Saul provides it by tearing off his surgical mask so that "his face was shining and his eyes were shining." In "triumph"—over himself?—he brings the work's ending back to the particular: "Mordeen, *I love my son*."

8

A page before this final outburst, Joe Saul had shouted out the nature of his discovery about humankind: *"There is a shining."* In so doing, he brings about an ending typical of so many of Steinbeck's writings, as noted earlier—and not merely the final ones, such as *East of Eden* and *The Winter of Our Discontent*. These epiphanies may or may not seem gratuitous to the reader, but especially in the later fictions, they constitute a state of satori, enlightenment.

The difference in the later works is that they happen to characters with whom Steinbeck clearly identifies: Joe Saul, Cal Trask and his narrator-creator, and Ethan Allen Hawley. They are accompanied by a change in novelistic voice, as though Steinbeck—without Ed Ricketts—had discovered how to speak in the first person at last. In *Burning Bright*, Steinbeck reached a crucial point: he had found a balance between a sense of being like everyone else and a way of asserting his specialness. At last—unlike Arthur Miller's Willy Loman—he knew who he was.

—JOHN DITSKY

Suggestions for Further Reading

Astro, Richard. *John Steinbeck and Edward F. Ricketts: The Shaping of a Novelist.* Minneapolis: University of Minnesota Press, 1974.

Benson, Jackson J. *The True Adventures of John Steinbeck, Writer.* New York: The Viking Press, 1984.

Britch, Carroll, and Clifford Lewis. Jackson J. Benson, ed. "*Burning Bright*: The Shining of Joe Saul." In *The Short Novels of John Steinbeck: Critical Essays with a Checklist to Steinbeck Criticism,* 217–34. Durham, NC: Duke University Press, 1990.

Bronson, Orval. *Burning Brightly: John Steinbeck on Stage.* Grass Valley, CA: Comstock Bonanza Press, 2000.

DeMott, Robert. *Steinbeck's Reading: A Catalogue of Books Owned and Borrowed.* New York: Garland Publishing, 1984.

Ditsky, John. Donald R. Noble, ed. "'I Know It When I Hear It on Stage': Theatre and Language in Steinbeck's *Burning Bright*." In *The Steinbeck Question: New Essays in Criticism,* 223–38. Troy, NY: Whitston Publishing, 1993.

Ditsky, John. *John Steinbeck and the Critics.* Rochester, NY: Camden House, 2000.

———. "Ritual Murder in Steinbeck's Dramas." *Steinbeck Quarterly* 11 (Summer/Fall 1978): 72–76.

———. "'Stupid Sons of Fishes': Shared Values in John Steinbeck and the Musical Stage," *Steinbeck Studies* 15 (Winter 2004): 107–16.

Fensch, Thomas. *Steinbeck and Covici: The Story of a Friendship.* Middlebury, VT: Paul S. Eriksson, 1979.

Gladstein, Mimi. Jackson J. Benson, ed. "Straining for Profundity: Steinbeck's *Burning Bright* and *Sweet Thursday*." In *The Short Novels of John Steinbeck: Critical Essays with a Checklist to Steinbeck Criticism,* 234–48. Durham, NC: Duke University Press, 1990.

Li, Luchen. ed. *Dictionary of Literary Biography,* Volume 309: *John Steinbeck:A Documentary Volume.* Detroit: Thomson Gale, 2005.

McElrath, Joseph, Jesse S. Crisler, and Susan Shillinglaw, eds. *John Steinbeck:The Contemporary Reviews.* New York: Cambridge University Press, 1996.

McPheron, William. *John Steinbeck: From Salinas to Stockholm.* Palo Alto, CA: Stanford University Libraries, 2000.

Nakayama, Kiyoshi. Susan Shillinglaw and Kevin Hearle, eds. "Novella into Play: *Burning Bright.*" In *Beyond Boundaries: Rereading John Steinbeck,* 151–61. Tuscaloosa: University of Alabama Press, 2002.

Parini, Jay. *John Steinbeck:A Biography.* New York: Henry Holt, 1995.

Railsback, Brian. Michael J. Meyer, ed. "The Bright Failure: What Shall We Make of Chaos? In *The Betrayal of Brotherhood in the Works of John Steinbeck: Cain Sign,* 327–56. Lewiston, NY: The Edwin Mellen Press, 2000.

Schultz, Jeffrey and Luchen Li. *Critical Companion to John Steinbeck:A Literary Reference to His Life and Work.* New York: Checkmark Books, 2005.

Sheffield, Carlton. Terry White, ed. Introduction by R. A. Blum. *John Steinbeck, The Good Companion.* Berkeley, CA: Creative Arts, 2002.

Shillinglaw, Susan, ed. *John Steinbeck: Centennial Reflections by American Writers.* San Jose, CA: San Jose State University Center for Steinbeck Studies, 2002.

Simmonds, Roy S. *A Biographical and Critical Introduction of John Steinbeck.* Lewiston, NY: The Edwin Mellen Press, 2000.

Steinbeck, John. Thomas Fensch, ed. *Conversations with John Steinbeck.* Jackson: University Press of Mississippi, 1988.

———. "Critics, Critics, Burning Bright." *The Saturday Review* 33 (November 11, 1950): 20–21; reprinted in *Steinbeck and His Critics:A Record of Twenty-Five Years,* 43–47. E. W. Tedlock and C. V. Wicker, eds. Albuquerque: University of New Mexico Press, 1957.

Steinbeck, John. Florian J. Shasky and Susan F. Riggs, eds. Foreword by Carlton Sheffield. *Letters to Elizabeth:A Selection of Letters from John Steinbeck to Elizabeth Otis.* San Francisco: Book Club of California, 1978.

Steinbeck, John. Elaine Steinbeck and Robert Wallsten, eds. *Steinbeck: A Life in Letters.* New York: The Viking Press, 1975.

Steinbeck, John IV, and Nancy Steinbeck. Foreword by Andrew Harvey. *The Other Side of Eden: Life with John Steinbeck.* Amherst, NY: Prometheus Books, 2001.

Takamura, Hiromasa. *John Steinbeck and His Dramatic World.* Okayama, Japan: Nishi-Nippon Houki Publishing Company, 2001.

Burning Bright

ACT ONE

The Circus

The canvas walls of the dressing tent were discolored with brown water spots, with green grass stains and grey streaks of mildew, and the prickles of sun glittering came through. On the ground the close-cut barley stubble stood in bunches with the black 'dobe earth between. Near to one cloth wall there was a large and travel-beaten trunk with dull brass straps and corners, its lid upraised and a mirror the whole size of the top disclosed.

Joe Saul sat on a folding canvas chair before the trunk. He was naked to the waist but he had on tights and slippers. He dabbed the yellow powder on his face and painted his eyes with black——not carefully.

A lithe and stringy man of middle age, Joe Saul. His jaws muscled against strain and cables down the sides of his neck. His arms were white and blue-veined, with the long cords of clinging and hanging rather than the lumps of lifting. His hands were white, the fingers spatulate, and palms and fingers calloused from the rope and bar.

Joe Saul's face was rough and a little pockmarked; his eyes looked large and dark and glittering within their penciled edges. He finished his make-up and took a little bottle of dark hair dye from the trunk, poured some on a brush and worked the stain into his thick, graying hair, particularly at the temples. Then neatly he packed his powder and bottles back in the trunk and slipped on the shirt of his tights and cinched his canvas belt. Only a small bulge showed over the belt. He leaned back in his chair and flexed his hands, so that the thin muscles of his forearms squirmed.

From outside the dressing room came sounds of the developing show—call of barker and skirl of calliope and thin waltz of merry-go-round backed by the chutter of gathering people. And nearer sounded grunts of lions and whoosh of elephants, grunt and squeal of pigs and discontented snort of horses against the brass wail of a circus trombone.

And Joe Saul flexed his hands and looked down at them. From outside the flap came three short whistles in place of knocking.

"Come in," said Joe Saul, and Friend Ed stepped through the flap. Friend Ed was broader, taller, heavier, than Joe Saul, slower in motion and speech. He was dressed and made up too, a big pants clown ruffed at neck, wrists, and ankles, white suit with big red polka dots, and feet as long and curved as barrel staves: a white face, red rubber nose, sad black mouth and black lines over the eyelids. High on his forehead were painted the inverted V's of astonishment. He had created on his face a look of surprised perplexity. Only his thick dark hair and hands were his own. He carried the bald head with fringe of bright red hair and the big false hands.

Joe Saul closed the trunk lid to make a place for him to sit, and Friend Ed dropped his hair piece and his false hands on the trunk and seated himself on its edge and swung his big floppy clown foot gently back and forth.

"Where's Mordeen?" he asked.

"She went to sit with Mrs. Malloy's baby," said Joe Saul. "Mrs. Malloy's gone off to the post office to send a money order to her son Tom," he said monotonously. "Her son Tom, '*my-son-Tom.*' He's in college, you know." Joe Saul sat up tight-straight. "I'm sure, Friend Ed, I don't tell you for the first time that Mrs. Malloy has got a son Tom that's in college and only nineteen. Did you hear about that, Friend Ed? Did you hear about it twenty thousand times?"

Friend Ed opened his black mouth so that the red inner lips and little white teeth showed. "Don't curse him, Joe Saul," he said. "Or her."

"Who's cursing?" Joe Saul leaned back and flexed his hands on his knees. "She's a nice woman," he said. "And I guess if you've got a son Tom in college you've got a little fringe of God Almighty on your head, but I wouldn't curse her. I'm glad for her. She's a nice woman."

"Now look, Joe Saul, you're nervy."

"No."

Friend Ed glanced down at the flexing hands.

"That's a new thing, you're doing there. That's a nervy thing." His foot stopped its swinging.

Joe Saul looked at his hands. "I didn't know I was doing it," he said. "But you are right, Friend Ed. I've got a rustle in me. It's a little itching rustle under my skin."

"I see it coming on you, Joe Saul. It's not a thing of surprise to me except it's late. It's very late—I wonder why so late. Three years it is since Cathy died. You were strong in your wife-loss. You were not nervy then. And it's eight months since Cousin Will missed the net. You were not nervy then. Victor's a good partner, isn't he? You said he was. And it's not the first time a Saul missed the net in all the generations. What's the matter with you, Joe Saul? You're putting an itch in the air around you like a cloud of gnats in a hot evening."

Joe Saul flexed his hands, looked at them, and then he grappled them together to keep them still. "Victor's all right," he said. "Maybe better than Cousin Will. It's what you get used to. I could feel the tuning of Cousin Will. I knew his breathing and his pulse. Cousin Will was my blood and my being; we were the products of a thousand years, the end products. I have to think about Victor, think about what he'll do. I could feel Cousin Will in my nerve ends. Maybe I'll get used to Victor, but he's a stranger. His blood is not my blood. He has no ancestry in it."

Outside the tent a band struck up, playing an overture fast and hot.

"Is Mordeen made up, Joe Saul?"

"Sure. She wouldn't have gone else." His hands flexed again in spite of him, and Friend Ed noticed it.

"Is it your nerve? I've seen that happen. Do you fear for your hands? I knew a man once going blind and he ran about looking at color, looking and staring so he'd remember. He was afraid he might forget what color was like when he was blind. Do your hands trouble you?"

"I don't think so. Why should they? They've never slipped or lost their grip."

Friend Ed leaned over and touched Joe Saul on the shoulder. "Do I have the friend-right to ask a question, Joe Saul?"

"Always."

"Is there any trouble with Mordeen?"

"No—oh, no!"

"You're sure?"

"I'm—sure."

"It's a fine girl, Joe Saul, a fine wife. See you remember it. She's young—but very good. See you never doubt that. No man ever had better. Don't compare her with your Cathy—she's different but just as good, and lovely and true."

"I know."

"What I came to say is this. I'm having a little birthday party for the twins. They wanted only kids, but they asked for you and for Mordeen. Will you come and bring some little twist of a present?"

"Do they really ask for me?"

"They did—and will you keep your goddamned hands still?"

Joe Saul leaped up, and his slippers rustled in the stubble. He paced, holding his hands against their restlessness in front of him. He bit his underlip.

Friend Ed spoke quietly. "I'll take some of the itch from you, if you'll let me. I held you weeping when your Cathy died. I lifted Cousin Will off the ring rim, and I stood left hand to you with Mordeen. I think I know your sickness but you will have to say it first, Joe Saul."

The pacing stopped. "She's taking a long time to get a money order," he said. "I think you do know. I think your twins know. I wonder—whether Mordeen knows."

"Will you say it, then, for your mind's rest and your hands' peace? Maybe there's some kind of answer."

Joe Saul sighed. "I wonder is it age coming on me? I think of old times. They say old men think back. I think of my grandfather talking—that was after his hands were gone weak, and his timing gone and the certainty of his eye. When it didn't matter any more, he'd drink wine in the afternoon. He'd lesson us on the training mat, and when we were resting sometimes Grandfather would talk. He did a lot of reading, that old man, and more thinking. Maybe he made up things, but we believed him. You never knew him, Friend Ed."

"No, I never knew him. Talk it out, Joe Saul! Let's find the bitter seed that's like the inside of a peach pit."

Joe Saul sat in his chair and leaned back, thinking. "We were real proud kids," he said, "with one hip up and our chests stuck out. We believed everything he said because he was Old Joe Saul. I'm named for him. He used to say that we were nature spirits once—you know, in trees and streams. We lived in the wind and in the black storms. 'That's what your great-granddads were,' he'd say. Remember how white his hair was? No—you never saw him. Then he said we were the first doctors, but witch doctors. We troubled the waters and drove the thunder back over the edge, and we jumped like the streams over rocks, and we sailed— arms out—like the wind.

"Well, then he said we were doctors against hurt, and we had to make the form of hurt and sickness to drive it out, so that we were crooked for fits and spastic for poison, and we bent like rubber for a broken leg. He had it all down, and we'd squat and listen on the training mat." And Joe Saul squatted beside his chair to show how it was.

"It's a strange telling for children," Friend Ed interposed. "Would you sometime tell it to the twins?"

"Of course I will. The twins have the blood. They'd understand. Old Joe Saul said then in Greece we wore high shoes and wooden masks and we were gods. He said in Rome we tumbled in the red sand of the arena after the blood had run, and we juggled burning sticks in front of the set-up crosses and their burdens.

"Then in the dark centuries, he said, we laughed

and played in the miracles, and we were the only gay in that laughter-starving time. From then on, he said, everybody knows."

"I'll want the twins to hear," said Friend Ed.

"I told you he'd drink a little in the afternoon when he didn't go up any more and it didn't matter. Kings, he'd say, princes, counts, Astors, Vanderbilts, or Tudors, Plantagenets, Pendragons for that matter—who knows their great-granddads with any certainty? Old Joe Saul would stand there, tall and one finger out like a dry stick. He had a full head of hair and every tooth his own. He'd stand there, a white cloud, and we were proud kids squatting on the mat, all knee and elbow burned from the workout.

" 'Two ancient families there are,' he'd say, 'known and sure and recognized—and only two. Clowns and acrobats. The rest are newcomers.' "

Friend Ed breathed deep with satisfaction. "You can tell the twins at their birthday party, after the cake."

Joe Saul's face twisted with remembering now. He stood and his hands went to their gripping. "And he'd say to us, 'Have kids—have lots of kids! Be not ever without a baby on the fingers, a child on the mat, and a boy on the bar.' He'd scowl down on us sitting there."

Joe Saul was silent, and Friend Ed was silent. The sound of lightly tripping, snorting ring horses came through the tent. Friend Ed looked strongly at Joe Saul. "There's your bitter seed," he said. "There it is. Cathy had no child—but Mordeen?"

"It's been three years," Joe Saul said. "Three years."

"Do you begin to think it's you?"

"I don't know what it is—I don't know what it is. But a man can't die this way."

"Nor a woman either."

Joe Saul cried, "A man can't scrap his blood line, can't snip the thread of his immortality. There's more than just my memory. More than my training and the remembered stories of glory and the forgotten shame of failure. There's a trust imposed to hand my line over to another, to place it tenderly like a thrush's egg in my child's hand. You've given your blood line to the twins, Friend Ed. And now—three years with Mordeen."

"Maybe it's you should go to doctors. There might be a remedy you haven't thought of."

"What do they know?" Joe Saul cried. "There's some dark kind of curse on me, and I feel it."

"On you alone, Joe Saul?" Friend Ed smiled. "Do you feel singled out, pinned up alone in a museum? It's time we sing this trouble out into the air and light. Else it will grow with poisoned fingers like a cancer in your mind. Rip off the cover. Let it out! Maybe you're not alone in your secret cave."

"I know!" Joe Saul said quietly. "I guess I'm getting that way—digging like a mole into my own darkness. Of course, Friend Ed, I know it is a thing that can happen to anyone in any place and time—a farmer or a sailor, or a lineless, faceless Everyone! I know this—

and maybe all of these have the secret locked up in loneliness."

"That would do it. And now that I know, I'll try to help. I'll try to think—and help."

Suddenly Joe Saul said nervously, "I wonder what's keeping Mordeen. That's a long time to get a money order. Her baby—Mrs. Malloy's too old to have a baby. She's too old—she's forty-five."

"But she had it," said Friend Ed. And automatically to an unseen, unheard cue he put his hair piece on and smoothed the bald skin over his thick hair and patted the edges down on his forehead just above the incredulous eyebrows. "Now that I know, Joe Saul, I'll try to help. I'm on—" He put on his false hands, shuffled his big feet in a mincing dance step, and flopped out of the tent.

Joe Saul lifted the lid of the trunk and pulled his little chair close and peered at himself in the mirror. He leaned close and inspected his face. Suddenly Friend Ed looked in again. "I didn't mean that—I didn't mean it that way."

"Mean what?"

"I heard it in my ears, the way it sounded when I said, 'But she had it.' I didn't mean it that way, Joe Saul."

"I didn't hear it—that way," Joe Saul said uneasily. "You're on, Friend Ed." And sure enough, the shrill band played the march of elephants and white horses, giraffes and hippopotamuses and pinwheeling clowns. Friend Ed whirled, and the canvas dropped behind him.

He called a greeting outside. "Run, Mordeen, he's waiting for you."

Now the flap lifted and Mordeen came in. Her tights were white and silver and over her shoulders she wore a long silver and blue cape which fell in heavy folds to her ankles. Mordeen was fair and very beautiful, her golden hair in short tight curls, her eyes blued, her make-up carefully applied. She was smiling, her face alight with a pleasant memory.

Joe Saul swung around to her, his face dark and serious. "Have you seen Victor, Mordeen?"

"No, I haven't. That baby, Joe Saul, he crows, really crows, and rocks back and forth. He grabbed at a shaft of sunshine with his hand. You should have seen his face when his hand went through it, amazed and disappointed all at once." She laughed and then, seeing him and his posture, "What's the matter, Joe Saul? Aren't you well?"

"I'm all right." He stood up.

"Angry then? You must be angry. Your eyes are so black, but when you are angry they seem to have a red glow. Are you angry with me, Joe Saul?"

He moved very quickly to her and put his arms around her, and there was hunger and eagerness in his body and in his face.

"Not angry," he said. "No, not angry—and still angry." He stroked her cheek. "Angry at Time when you were away. Angry at Time. Irritated with the minutes when you aren't with me."

"I like that," she said. "It's good to be missed. I

came back as soon as I could. It's good to be away a little. Then I know how well and strongly I love you."

He strained her tight to him. "I get frightened," he said. "My mind plays games. It whispers that you don't exist. It sneers that you have gone away. It whines to me that there is no Mordeen. It's a cruel, mischievous game."

She was smiling and her voice was sleepy, languorous. "It's a child's game to make good things better," she said. "I remember holding a piece of white cake with black frosting and pretending it was not mine. That was to make it nicer when I tasted it. Now, Joe Saul, that's better. The red is gone out of your eyes. You have the blackest eyes—like new split coal—that black! But you were angry, or very troubled."

"If I was, I am not now," he said. "Everything bad evaporates when I touch you. I love you, Mordeen—starvingly."

"Then you are not satisfied?"

"No—never—I never am. What a dull thing that would be—like the slight, painful sluggishness of an overfull stomach, like too much food or too much sleep. No, you keep me fed and hungry, and that is the best."

She pushed him a little bit away from her so she could look clearly into his face. "Will you tell me what is worrying you, Joe Saul?"

"It's nothing," he said.

"Is it Victor?"

"A little."

"Is it—" she paused—"anything else?"

"No—no."

"Am I a good woman to you?"

He held her tight. "Oh, my God! My God, Mordeen! You're a burning flower in my heart. See—I am harsh breathing like a boy. I'm full of you."

The flap opened again and Victor entered. Joe Saul released Mordeen, slowly and proudly, and turned to face him.

Victor was large and powerful, dark and young. His mouth was full and arrogant, his eyes sullen. He wore flannel slacks and a white T-shirt, and a gold medallion on a golden chain hung at his throat. His skin bloomed with youth. He held his right arm across his stomach, and the wrist was tightly bandaged with surgical tape. He stood defiantly in the entrance. Mordeen slipped quietly around until she stood behind Joe Saul.

As for Joe Saul, he stared at Victor, first with perplexity and then with growing anger.

"Why aren't you ready?" he asked, and then he saw the tape. "What's that?"

Victor put threat and self-sufficiency on his face to cover fear. "I sprained my wrist," he said. "I just came from the doctor."

For a long moment Joe Saul regarded him and then he asked very quietly, "How?"

Victor expected anger. He was not prepared for quietness—he was not braced for quietness. He had been set and poised to repel a rage, he carried rage to defend himself. In the ominous quiet he was off balance and he could not change his pattern of defense.

"No need to get mad," he said loudly. "I couldn't help it. I tell you it was an accident. Might happen to anybody—might happen any time."

Joe Saul turned slowly back and forth like a gun turret, and he was silent. But Victor blustered on. "I was playing, just playing around with some of the fellows—touch football. That's all, just playing, and one guy just put out his foot—didn't mean it. Say, what's the matter with you?" He shifted back uneasily, for Joe Saul had stood up and moved slowly near to him. And Joe Saul's voice recited without rise or fall, monotonously.

"You went to high school in a little town," he said. "Ohio, was it?" He did not wait for an answer. "Athlete, half mile, pole vault, tumbling team. And funny —like a clown. And everyone said that you should be on the stage, wasting your time there in the little town. Ran away with a circus—the old dream, every little boy's escape."

He stopped and licked his lips.

And Victor said, "The doctor says three days. It's only a strained tendon. What are you yelling about?"

Joe Saul went on quietly as though he had not heard. "It isn't that you didn't know but that you can't ever know. If you were a musician, you'd bat a tennis ball with your violin. If you were a surgeon, you'd sharpen pencils with a scalpel."

Victor said, "Don't shout at me!"

Joe Saul said quietly, "It sounds like that to you, does it? You're stronger, quicker, younger, even more sure than Cousin Will, but now I know what it is. Whatever you do is an accident of youth and muscle. You have not the infinite respect for your tools and your profession—Profession! You have made it a trade."

Joe Saul's tone had sharpened in contempt. "And you have not even learned your trade. You did not hang clinging to your father's forefingers. You have no blood in it." He paused uneasily and looked away.

Mordeen moved closer to him, shivering a little at his quietness. And her movement caught Victor's attention and gave him his weapon. Almost with relief he put her up as a shield against the lashing.

"What's the matter—feeling old?" His eyes went to meet Mordeen.

Joe Saul asked blankly, "What?"

Victor pressed forward, like a yammering boy after a hurt cat. "What's the matter—jealous? What's the matter—afraid you can't keep up with a young girl? Is she too much for you?"

Joe Saul was staring at the ground. He sighed and he said softly, "I'll go and report that we can't go on for three days." Slowly he moved very near and struck Victor hard in the face with his open palm. Then he turned and walked lightly on his toes out of the dressing tent.

Mordeen went quickly to the open trunk, dropped

her cape over the little chair, sat down and rubbed cold cream on her face. But Victor stood in shock, unable to get over the nausea of the insult. His eyes were glazed with hatred and the inability to put it to violent use. He moved dumbly, nearer to Mordeen.

"I couldn't hit an old man, a man old enough to be my father," he said.

Mordeen rubbed the cold cream into her skin and wiped it off on a little towel. She did not look around.

"You notice I didn't raise a hand against him?" Victor said. "He knew he was safe. He knew I wouldn't hit him back—an old man like that."

"He can't hear you," Mordeen said. She wiped the eye shadow from around her eyes.

"I wouldn't care if he could. You heard me say the same thing right in his face."

"And I saw what he did to you," said Mordeen.

"I could break him with my hands," said Victor, and with his hands he showed how he could do it. "I could throw him like an old sack. Why, I could crush him—but I didn't. That wouldn't be fair."

Mordeen turned toward him. The yellow and blue and red streaked towel was in her hand. "You're really afraid of him," she said softly.

Victor surged toward her, his chest up and the muscles rippling on his shoulders. "How do you mean afraid? I tell you I could tear him apart."

Mordeen looked at him for a long minute. "Why didn't you then?" she asked.

"Because—" He fought the question because he did not know. Then he formed his answer. His voice grew silky. "Because—I'll tell you why. I have respect for you." He considered his solution. "Because I don't want trouble or fighting when there's a girl I—i am in love with."

Mordeen looked up at him in wonder. "In love with?" Her mouth stayed open after she had said it.

Victor moved closer. He put out his hand to touch her shoulder, but when she looked at his hand he took it away. "I didn't tell you," he said. "I tried to keep it in. I want to be fair. I'm not the kind of guy that creeps on his partner. But he hit me—in the face."

Mordeen said quietly, "You hit him below the belt. That's how fair you are."

Victor began, "I didn't lay a hand—oh, yes," he said, chuckling, "I see what you mean. That got him, didn't it? Next time he whips out that tongue of his, I'll get him again. I know how—now." His lips curled with hatred. He was poisoned with insult. "I don't need to hit him. I can just stand back and punch him with a word. He's old, and you can't get cured of that."

Mordeen smiled up at him. "Besides, you respect and love me," she said sardonically.

Victor shook his head, like a bruised fighter with a steady left hand in his face. And suddenly he fell back on the surest defense there is—none. It was a wrestling tactic to go limp against strain. "I'm a fool," Victor said. "Joe Saul is right. I don't know my ass from a teacup. Of course he's right. But maybe I'll learn. Maybe I'll grow up someday." His face was young and eager. "I admire Joe Saul more than anybody in the world. That's why it hurt so much when he hit me the way you'd hit a dog. That's why I hit back—because I was hurt. That's why I did it.

"Let's start fresh, Mordeen. I'll apologize to Joe Saul. He'll understand why I did it when I tell him how hurt I was. I don't know my ass from a teacup. Coming from high school, being with famous people, trying to be like them when I don't know enough. Why, it's a privilege to be taught by Joe Saul. I know it. I'm sorry I lost myself, Mordeen."

She watched him, believing and not believing, and then deciding to believe because she couldn't see what there was to lose. "I can see how that is," she said. "Oh, I've had things like that happen to me, things that made me dumb and sick. You see, Victor, we're a kind of a little world inside a world. We have a whole life and pattern most people just don't know about. Lots of people resent us or envy us. And so we're proud and maybe a little bit afraid of people. Maybe we protect ourselves too much."

"I see what you mean," he said, although he didn't at all.

"When you argue with a child," she said warmly, "you give a good argument and the child says yah, yah! You understand him and he doesn't listen, so the child wins."

"I see what you mean," he said softly. A little purr crept into his voice. She looked up for a moment in apprehension. "I see what you mean," he repeated, and the purr was gone.

He hurried on. "I never think of you growing up —here."

"But I did." Her voice was very soft. "My whole life. I was born in a sleeping car, raised in the ring. I rode in a hoodah before I could walk."

Victor's unfortunate choice it was always to mis-see, to mis-hear, to misjudge. He read softness into her because of the softness of her voice, when she was only remembering. His was the self-centered chaos of childhood. All looks and thoughts, loves and hatreds, were directed at him. Softness was softness toward him, weakness was weakness in the face of his strength. He preheard answers and listened not. He was full colored and brilliant—all outside of him was pale.

"You knew Joe Saul's first wife?" he asked.

"Oh, yes."

"Did Joe Saul love her?"

"Oh, yes! Oh, very yes."

He paused and his lashes fell over his fine eyes. He droped on one knee so that his eye level was a little below hers. He studied her face, or seemed to—brows, eyes, nose, upper lip well bowed, lower lip full and passionate, tight with exquisite nerves. He spoke softly but with the purr of insinuation in his voice.

"Why did you marry him?"

She raised her head, astonished. "Why?"

"Yes, why? A fifty-year-old man, or nearly, a man near-finished when you've only started. Why did you marry him?"

Mordeen smiled then with kindness at him, smiled almost with affection, as one does when a little boy first asks, "What is God?"

"I married him because—because I loved him."

"That was three years ago. Do you love him now?"

Her lips stood apart as though she listened to faintly heard music outside a summer window. "More," she said. "Much more."

He brought his malformed wisdom, his pool-hall, locker-room, jokebook wisdom to the front. "Joe Saul must be like a father in your mind," he said meanly.

"Oh, no."

He laughed. "I know more about women than you give me credit for," he said. "Isn't it true—you don't have to answer, you don't have to say anything—isn't it true that you sometimes wish for, maybe even crave, the hard arms of a young man and the smooth skin of a young man"—his voice rose—"the force, and body lust, and crushing passion of a young man?"

"No," she said softly. "That is not true. That is not true."

"I don't believe you," he said. "I know more than that."

Her kindness toward him lasted on as though there were enough warm blanket over her life so that she could spare a corner for his shoulders.

"I guess you really don't believe me," she said. "Maybe that will be your sorrow. Maybe sometime in a cold perplexity you'll wonder what you missed, and maybe you'll only be dimly aware of missing something."

"I'm not a baby," he cried. "I've been around. I've known women."

"Happy women?"

"When I got through with them they were happy."

"For how long?"

He boasted, "They weren't happy until they could have me again. They always wanted me again."

"Of course. And they'll be wondering what they missed. I'm not telling any secret—Joe Saul knows that I had some other life. I know the tricks, techniques of duration, of position, games, perverse games to drive the nerves into a kind of hysterical laughter."

Victor's mouth was wet now, and he breathed through his mouth and his tongue went over his lips. "I told you I didn't believe you."

She said, "Joe Saul knows one trick, one ingredient. You haven't heard about it. Maybe you never will. Without that trick you'll one day go screaming silently in loss. Without it there are no good methods or techniques. You know I've wondered how it is that one act can be ugly and mean and enervating, like a punishing drug, and also most beautiful and filled with energy, like milk."

Victor stood up and he spoke with uneasy truculence. "What is this trick that makes a young girl fall in love with Old Joe Saul? Do you think he can do anything I can't do?"

"Yes."

"What is this ingredient?"

"Affection," she said softly. "You have never learned it. Very many people never do."

Victor was uneasy, and he felt failure—that he had been caught in a failure. He said loudly, "You mean I'm not as good a man as Old Joe Saul? Let me try, and I swear to God you'll never go back to him. Ah! we're all alike, men, women. What are you telling me? A jump in the hay is a jump in the hay. What's this breathless thing?"

"All alike," she said. "Surely—all alike. And everyone who hammers out a tune makes great music, and when one rough line rhymes with another that's great poetry, and every daub on canvas is a great painting."

"What are you getting at?" he asked uneasily.

Mordeen said, "I used to wonder why this love seemed sweeter than I had ever known, better than many people ever know. And then one day the reason came to me. There are very few great Anythings in the world. In work and art and emotion—the great is very rare. And I have one of the great and beautiful. Now say your yah, yah, Victor, like a child unanswerably answering Wisdom. You will have to do that, I think."

Victor said, "If it's so goddam good, why does he have the jerks? Why does he go stepping around like a cat on hot rocks? Why's his temper short and the gray coming into his sick face? Tell me that if it's so goddam good."

Mordeen had become rigid, her mouth tight and her eyes veiled.

"You do have a gift," she said. "Instinctively you know where to put the knife and how to twist it. I know what you mean, but you don't know. You groped blindly and found a thing as precious as a porcelain doorknob in the dark." She stood up and stepped close to him. Her face was cold and her voice icy. "I want to tell you this," she said. "Maybe I'm telling myself. I will do anything—anything—anything to bring content to him. See you remember that, Victor."

His guard was up now and he wasn't listening; he was only angry because here was a world he could not enter and so he had to disbelieve in its existence. He fell back on the world he knew. He said, "You're setting yourself high. What makes you so special?"

"Joe Saul," she said quickly.

"You're a woman like any other woman—same equipment, no more, no less. Everything else is the same too. You need what every girl in the world needs—a little bit of forcing so you can claim it wasn't your fault. Maybe you need the back of the hand, maybe you need—" He grabbed her in his arms, holding her elbows against her sides. "Maybe you need— me." He leaned over to kiss her and she sagged and relaxed so that, holding her, he could not reach her mouth with his mouth. Her head fell limply away from him and her body hung dead in his arms.

Victor was puzzled now. He had instinctively pinned her arms against resistance. Her eyes were closed, and she was still. Outside the tent flap there were three short whistles instead of knocking. But neither Victor nor Mordeen heard. The whistles were repeated, and then Friend Ed stepped through the flap. His make-up was off but he still wore his polka-dot clown suit. He stood looking at Victor's back. Then slowly he moved toward them.

Victor was worried. "Mordeen," he said, "Mordeen, are you all right?" He released his arms, and as he did, she stepped quickly back away from him. Her face was snarling with hatred and contempt. Then she saw Friend Ed and she stared at him.

Victor looked around and his hand went up protectively. Friend Ed stepped closer. "Go away," he said softly. "Go away now! I'll never tell. I think Joe Saul would kill you."

Victor said, "I didn't—"

"Go away. It wouldn't be good for Joe Saul to kill you—not good for Joe Saul. Even if they didn't catch him he'd carry a sourness all his life. You're not worth that much to him or to me. Tell him you have to leave the show—your mother died, anything. But go!"

"I—you don't know—"

Friend Ed dropped his shoulders and moved closer. "Maybe I'll have to take the sourness myself. Please, please go away!"

Victor said, "Nobody can make me go away." He looked at his taped wrist. "You watch yourself."

"All right, but go away now, go away."

Victor hesitated. "Don't think I'm afraid," he said, but he walked to the flap and disappeared.

Mordeen and Friend Ed watched him go and then they turned sluggishly and looked at each other, and they seemed to look through cloudy water so that they had to stare to see at all. A wall of slowness separated them.

Mordeen said in a dreaming voice, "You saw all that, Friend Ed?"

"Yes, I saw."

"What do you believe?"

"I believe what I saw."

"Do you think Joe Saul would?"

"He would want to—he would have to, and if he couldn't I would try to make him."

Mordeen sighed deeply. She said, "Victor knowing nothing and feeling very little has an instinct for finding frail places and areas of pain. I'm sure he doesn't know anything, and still he feels and probes like a blind leech and he gets blood."

Friend Ed looked at her for a long moment. "Joe Saul reported the act couldn't go on and then he went to a bar. He's getting drunk, Mordeen."

She sat down wearily, started to speak. "I must—" and she was silent.

"Do you want to talk to me?" Friend Ed asked.

"Yes—yes, I do. There's a cloud coming down. I

want to talk. He's getting drunk. Is that part of the cloud?"

"Do you know what the cloud is?"

"Yes. Do you?"

"Yes."

Friend Ed asked quickly, "Will you tell me this: can you have a baby?"

Mordeen looked away from him. "Yes, I can."

"How do you know?"

"The only way I could know. I know."

"When did it happen?"

"Five years ago."

"Does Joe Saul know?"

"No, he doesn't. It was before. It was all dead and done, before Joe Saul."

Friend Ed said, "I don't understand it. He hasn't never been sick that I know of. He's a twisting mass of strength and force."

She said softly, "He was sick once. He told me. It was the only time and when he was a boy. Growing pains, they called it. His bones and his joints ached and the fever burned him. For a year he was whipped with pain."

Friend Ed's eyebrows rose. "And you took his account and discovered—"

"Yes, rheumatic fever."

"And could that be the cause?"

"Yes," she said. "It could. It need not but it could." She said passionately, "Can't we tell him? Could we bring this in the open? We need a baby. We can get one, adopt it, and it will be ours. Maybe if this thing were certain and understood the cloud would go away. Maybe—"

"I don't think you can tell him that," Friend Ed said. "I don't think that would be good. Do you know what happens to a man when he knows he is sterile?"

"I know he is miserable now and hungry, starving for a child. I know it has always been, but now it's frantic."

"Is he a good lover?"

"Oh, wonderful! Gentle and fierce and—wonderful."

Friend Ed said quietly, "When the bodies of man and woman meet in love there is a promise—sometimes so deep buried in their cells that thinking does not comprehend—there is a sharp promise that a child may be the result of this earthquake and this lightning. This each body promises the other. But if one or the other knows—knows beyond doubt that the promise can't be kept—the wholeness is not there; the thing is an act, a pretense, a lie, and deeply deep, a uselessness, a thing of no meaning."

"I know," she said.

"How it is with a woman I'm not sure," he continued. "But with a man—perhaps he may feel free because he is in no danger; and perhaps the woman may feel wildly free in lust without consequence, but in her tissues there is contempt for a sterile man. And in a man there is a searching for the contempt he knows is there. Then, no matter how she pretends and protests and covers the sadness of the sterile love, he knows and feels it. And since we do not willingly do futile things, the man's body gradually refuses to perform a useless act, and the woman—oh, very slowly—has no need for him and her senses turn away from the dark double disappointment."

Mordeen looked down at her hands and she said, "I don't think that is so with me. I think I would do anything—anything my mind or heart or body can conceive—to give contentment to Joe Saul."

Friend Ed replied, "That is because he does not know. Once he knows—knows beyond every hiding, boding doubt that his seed is dead—he will not permit you even to try. The fog of his self-contempt will settle over him, and you will not be able ever to find him again in his gray misery."

"Then what should I do?" she asked.

"I don't know," he said. "It would be different if his mind and energy could rove creatively in the stars of mathematics or build out of eight notes a pattern of music new and living—then he might survive. But these things he does not have, and most men do not. Swinging on his high bar, timing his swing to catch your turning body—this is as old and instinctive to him as chewing when meat is in his mouth."

"What shall I do?"

"Don't make him know."

"But suppose it is not true. Suppose by some ac-

cident he became alive; suppose the fault is mine, an
organ disarranged, an acid improperly applied by my
own body, a poisoned thought lying concealed but
toxic."

"You don't believe that," Friend Ed said. "I know
you. You've had all the tests. You know."

She put her forehead in her hands. "Do you know
how I love this man, Friend Ed?"

"I think I do. I hope I do."

"Do you know I would protect him from hurt if I
were ripped and burned in the process?"

"That would be only a double burning."

"Do you know I am capable of any lie or cheat or
violence—any good or bad that a human can
conceive—for his content and joy?"

"I think you are. And I wonder what tiny mote of
chance there is of its succeeding."

She looked at him closely. "You know what I am
considering, don't you?"

"I think so."

"If I were very careful, took every precaution, don't
you think there is a possibility?"

"I can't advise you. I don't know."

"But without it what chance is there?"

"I don't know. I will not advise you. I might be
wrong."

"But of only two choices and both wrong, and one
long waiting and it wrong too—must I not choose the
least wrong of three?"

Friend Ed beat his hands together. "I don't know.

I tell you I will not advise you. I will not offer my responsibility, I will not endorse your note of happiness. Anything, anything else. I wish I didn't know, I wish I did not even a thread suspect what you are thinking and planning."

Mordeen sat very straight. "I know you are his friend," she said. "I suppose I put too much burden on friendship. It isn't a rope that can take that much strain. I should have made the pattern by myself, Friend Ed. But I was lonely and unsure. I thought I needed some strength outside myself to help me. I'm sorry."

"Then you will—"

"Hush," she said softly. "I will close everything away in a dark self. If I am wrong about anything it will be *my* wrongness, and you need not think it or touch it."

He bowed his head.

Mordeen said, "He would not like me to see him drunk, particularly if his drinking is not happy. Find him, Friend Ed, stay with him. And when he is tired beyond wakefulness, take him to the sleeping car and cover him well. See his clothes are off. You'll find his night things in the black case under the lower berth— and wind his watch—and see his chest is covered when he sleeps."

"You?" he asked.

"Oh, yes—tell him I had a little headache and I will walk for a while. Tell him I will come to him very soon."

"I'm afraid," he said.

"I was. I was more afraid than I have ever been in a small, terrified life. But now I am not. Maybe I needed your weakness to build my own strength. Go out and find Joe Saul and comfort him. Hurry! He might be in need. Hurry, Friend Ed. Change your clothes quickly and find him. Put him to sleep before the night show. Do this for us." She took him by the arm and led him to the flap and held it back for him. And Friend Ed went uncertainly away.

Then quickly she came back and leaned over the mirror in the trunk lid and brushed her short hair. She was putting on her lipstick when the flap opened and Victor stepped quietly in. Victor wore slacks and a bright shirt, a sport coat and a painted tie. His shoes were white and brown. Across his tie hung a gold chain from which a small gold football dangled. She saw him in the mirror of her trunk. She turned halfway toward him and spoke in flat, quick voice. "Why did you come back?"

He said sullenly, "Did you think I could be frightened away? No, I want to square things off. I followed Joe Saul into town and then came back. I waited for that one to go. I want to square some things away with you."

She made a great effort. "I'm sorry and ashamed, Victor. I was going to try to find you—to say I'm sorry."

He scowled at her. "What changed you then? Have

a fight with your old man? He's getting drunk, you know—or did you know?—pig drunk. I stood beside him in the bar, and he looked at me with juicy red eyes and he didn't even know me—that happy man, that good old lover with his trick."

"I'm sorry, Victor, really sorry."

"What changed you then?" he asked. "Did you suddenly find out that maybe I was right, that maybe this soggy stuff you thought was love might be a wizened imitation?"

"No, not quite that," she said.

"Or did you dig down through your pile of sticky words and find out that they were only words, when you needed hard and young action?"

"No, not quite that," she said.

"I came in to tell you once and finally what I think of the crap you were shoveling around. I want you to know that I won't have any of it. You were pretty tough, pretty sure. You know, you sit on the very peak top of the dunghill and look down on all the other chickens. You're perfect and me, I—I'm filth. Well, I tell you, I'm only honest. I'm not caught up in your stinking cloud." He paused and then continued, "And I don't believe you are either."

She said, "I was going to try to find you and tell you I was sorry."

"Why should you be sorry? What do you want of me?"

"After you left, I knew you were hurt," she said. "I told you how tight and clannish we are in this business. I'm afraid we have a way of rejecting everyone who was not born in it and descended from parents and grandparents who were born in it."

"You sure made me feel welcome!" he said sneeringly, and his eyes were very hostile.

"That's what I thought about," she said. "You are in our profession. If you stay you will have children born to it. We—I should not have cut you off the way I did. An act like ours is a kind of family, Victor. We—I should have made you feel more part of us."

"It's too late now. Your old man hit me in the face and you played dead, and the goddamned clown—did you hear what he said to me? Does he think I'll run away?"

"He didn't understand," she said. "Maybe we're so close-clotted that none of us understood. I'd like to make you feel welcome."

"How are you going to go about that?" he asked.

"I don't know," she said. "If we have hurt you so deeply, I don't know. I thought of a possible way, but I don't know."

He eyed her foxily and a secret triumph began to creep over him. He said vulgarly, "Well, I know one way you could make a start."

Her eyes were wide on him. "I would like to be friends with you, Victor. I mean that. And maybe the others—maybe I can help to make you welcome."

He came close to her. "I guess I don't care so much about the others."

"Yes, you do. I think you do. Victor, I thought of

something. When I was a little girl I had a time of sharp loneliness. I guess everyone has. I felt unwanted and cold, rejected. I took all the pennies I had and bought presents and wrapped them and gave them to myself. I thought that if the other children saw how I got presents they would know I was very popular and they would want to be my friends. But it didn't work. And then, Victor, an older girl got into trouble. She stole a ring. She was afraid and she was wary of the friends she had. She came to me for help, and I helped her, and —listen, Victor—I felt warm and wanted. I felt good when I could give something so frantically needed, and I was not lonely any more."

He said, "You're funny. You always tell stories. What's this one about? What do you want me to get from it? Your stories are loaded, Mordeen." But his voice had lost its sullenness. And he smiled a little in spite of himself. "Tell me," he said. "What's your story about?"

"Well," she began hesitantly, "it is about making you feel welcome. And I thought that if you would help me, when I need help, it might be good rich thing for both of us."

His truculence was going out of him and in spite of himself a jauntiness crept in. "Now who would think you needed help?" he said. "I thought I was the one needed help. That's what you said."

"Victor, you saw yourself that there is a trouble on us. Maybe if I could explain it so that you could understand it, you might be willing to help me." Her eyes appealed to him, and Victor went past understanding, went into triumph. He put his hand out to touch her shoulder—withdrew it when her shoulder moved imperceptibly away. Suddenly he laughed and his hand settled with authority on her shoulder.

"Why, I'd do anything for you, baby," he said. And then, "I'm sorry I was rough with you before. I know better than that. I guess I was afraid of you. I've got over that now." He stared at her. "Maybe you've changed. But they say women and horses know when a man isn't sure of himself. They can tell no matter how much he bluffs."

Mordeen's eyes veiled with pain, and she withdrew a little into herself. "I thought you might understand," she said softly.

"I do," he cried. "Christ, what a fool a man can be! I hear the signals, I see the lights, and I'm just dumb. I know a dame can't make the first move. How stupid can I be? Here you've thought it over, and I'm dragging my toe like a country boy."

He laughed again. "Let's get the hell out of here. Your old man's drunk. We'll go to a show. We'll go to town and have dinner. Say, how would it be if I rent a car and we go for a ride?"

Her face had tightened now. She turned away from him toward the trunk. She picked up a lipstick and drew on full lips. Her throat was tight, but she had made her decision. Her haggard face smoothed out

and imperceptibly her posture became soft and pro-
vocative.

"How about it?" he demanded.

When she turned to him again she was different.

"How about what, Victor?" she said huskily.

"How about dinner and we go for a ride?"

She looked up at him, studying his face. "That will
be very nice," she said. Her intonation had changed.
"I don't get out very much." She continued to stare at
him.

"What do you see?" he asked gaily.

"See? Oh, I was noticing how black your eyes are."

"Don't you like them?"

"Oh, yes. I was thinking how some families have
a black-eyed child and a blue-eyed child. It's strange."

"Not in my family," he crowed. "There hasn't
been a light eye on either side that anyone knows."

"That's strange," she said. "Families have such
strange qualities. I knew a family that had fits and, do
you know, in every second generation there was
insanity."

"You know funny people. I guess we're lucky. Old
age is the only thing that can kill us. My grandparents,
all four, are still alive, and my great-grandfather on my
father's side knocked off at a hundred and four. No,
we're tough. But what are we doing here? Let's get the
hell out of here."

"Yes," she said, "that will be nice." She stood up
and pulled her long cape over her shoulders. "I'll go
back to the sleeping car and dress," she said. "I'll have

to look nice. We'd better not be seen. Where can I meet you?"

He studied her. "No," he said slowly, "I guess you won't stand me up. Baby, there's a Chinese joint—nice booths. It's on Twelfth Street, but around the corner from the bank. It's like in an alley. I'll be in the first booth with the curtains drawn." He smiled down on her, his teeth flashing. "I'll take care of you, honey. I won't get you in any trouble. You just trust me."

She stood up and moved toward the flap. "Don't come out with me. I'll meet you in an hour." She stopped, and the spirit almost left her.

Victor stood beside her and he felt the change. He slipped his arm cozily about her waist. "I bet I know what you're thinking," he said. "Don't worry about it. We didn't invent this—it happens every day. It's nobody's fault. Don't you feel bad. Why, it can happen to anybody! We aren't so special. It can happen to anybody."

"Don't come out with me," she said.

She went out and left him. And almost instantly she was back. "He's coming. I saw him coming. Quick, get out! Quick!"

He went to the other side of the tent, lifted the canvas from the ground, and slipped underneath.

Mordeen breathed deeply. She parted the flap and looked out. She seemed about to go and then withdrew. But the next moment she was gone—gone in a flash.

The light was golden and soft now. The afternoon

slid down the tent. From outside, the circus band struck up the recessional march, and below the music there was the thud of elephants' feet and the whinnying of horses. A lion roared in hunger, and suddenly a whole family of pigs went squealing.

Then the tent flap opened and Joe Saul looked in. His eyes rolled vacantly and his mouth was wet and loose. His shoulders hung askew and his tie was crooked in his unbuttoned shirt collar.

"Mordeen," he said thickly. "Mordeen, I'm drunk. I'm sorry but I'm drunk." He peered at the trunk standing open. He staggered to the little chair and sat down. His hands fluttered lovingly over the trunk. He picked up her lipstick, smelled it, and he smiled. Clumsily he put the trunk in order and patted the tray that held the powder and grease paint and cold cream. He caught sight of himself in the mirror and stared at his loose, drunken face. Then suddenly he slammed the trunk lid shut. The tinkle of broken mirror sounded through its sides. He put his head down on his arm, cradled his face against his forearm. His right fist struck the trunk top hard, then more softly. "Mordeen," he said, "I hurt Friend Ed. Sent him away." His fist fell and the fingers slowly opened.

Friend Ed looked in at the flap. He saw Joe Saul, watched him a moment, and then entered silently. Friend Ed squatted down on the ground and crossed his ankles. He crossed his arms lightly and took up his vigil over Joe Saul.

ACT TWO

The Farm

The June morning sun peered over the ridgepole of the barn and fell across the farmhouse porch and tumbled bright and yellow through the windows into the kitchen. The light reflected from the polished metal of the stove and glittered on the pie tins set up in the warmer to dry. It was a kitchen to live in: a square table covered with oil cloth, for eating and figuring and sewing and reading; straight chairs with little pads in their seats for comfort; a big calendar from an implement house, but a calendar for keeping notes, with room around the dates to fill in plans projected for seeding and cultivating and harvesting. It was a self-sufficient kitchen. There was even a cot under the window where a tiring wife might rest while the bread was baking. On a shelf beside the sink stood a little radio playing the sprightly music of the morning, a record of a circus band playing a wild recessional.

This was a warm and old and comfortable kitchen, beaten into ease by generations. From outside came the farmyard noises of chickens cackling, of pigs grunting, of horses snorting and whinnying in their stalls. And a late rooster crowed as though he could not give up his morning song even though the sun was risen. A teakettle hummed steam on the stove, a coffee pot grunted and bumped beside it. The farm clock ticked, its pendulum flashing by the little glass window.

Joe Saul, the farmer, sat by the table, his head down on his elbow. His right hand held a pen, and in front of him was an open ink bottle. Friend Ed, who owned a neighboring farm, sat hunched down in a chair beside him. Both men were dressed in blue jeans and blue shirts open at the throat. Their coffee cups stood on the table in front of them.

Friend Ed got up and took his coffee cup to the stove and filled it. "Want a refill?" he asked.

Joe Saul raised his head and shoved his coffee cup over to the edge of the table. "Thanks," he said.

Friend Ed filled his cup. "You ought to get a book-keeper to do it for you. That's what I do. There's getting to be so much paper work a man hasn't time to bring in a crop."

Joe Saul sipped his coffee, then added sugar and cream. "When I can't keep books on my own farm I ought to give up farming," he said. "I've always been good at arithmetic, but there's just too much of it. But it's not only that. I've got to do everything myself—or at least be there."

"Isn't Victor working out?" Friend Ed asked.

"Oh, he's a good enough worker—tries anyway. But he's got no blood for it, Friend Ed. Before Cousin Will was killed I could send him out to cultivate and know and be sure it would be done right. But Victor's a town boy. Sometimes he does things right, but you can't be sure. I have to be with him all the time. You know how it is, Friend Ed, with you and me, and how it was with Cousin Will and our fathers and grand- and great- and great-great-grandfathers—we do things, and we don't know how or why but it's right. You can't be told about the land or read about it. It's got to be in the blood. I'm not criticizing Victor: he tries hard and mostly he's all right, but I just can't be sure. I've always got to go and look."

"I know," Friend Ed observed. "A funny thing happened like that with the twins. Al said at breakfast yesterday, 'I've got a feeling about something I should do.' And Eddie said, 'I know. Your green beans want poles.' Just like that, as if the green beans were calling to him."

"That's what I mean," Joe Saul said. "They've got the blood. You'd never have to look at a patch of corn if the twins did the hoeing. Oh, my God almighty!"

"Now stop this," Friend Ed said. "Now stop this! You're tearing yourself like a rupture."

Joe Saul said, "I get a nightmare sometimes. I see this land—this sweet flat black land—and in my nightmare it goes back to fallow, and then the sumac comes back in clumps, and then the forest trees, and this house molders away until there's only a chimney and cellar hole. The farm goes back the way it was when Old Joe Saul pulled up and took salt and pepper and tobacco, gunpowder and seed corn, from his saddlebags. That's all he had, Friend Ed, those and an ax. He cut five trees and planted his seed corn with a pointed stick. He used to tell about it when we were little kids tending our first calves." He gestured toward the door with his hand. "And look at it now—flat and black and sweet, shining like steel when the spring plow cuts in. And in ten years it could be nearly the way it was, with no one to keep it up. I get nightmares, too, of strangers— maybe from the towns, who don't know how to drain and damp."

"Stop it, Joe Saul. You worry at yourself like a puppy with a pig's ear. Get back to your paper work and stop mauling yourself. How's Mordeen?"

"Well, I don't know. She's a little sickly the last two weeks. There's one thing worries me, Friend Ed. She's had an ache or two before and you'd never know it. She's farm stock—get up and do her work and never a complaint or a shirk in her. And now—well, her stomach *is* upset, sure, and she's a little dizzy sometimes, but she's different. She went to the doctor yesterday. She says he told her it was nothing serious but she'd have to take it easy. It's funny. She's almost lah de dah! This morning she said, 'Would you mind if I didn't get up for a while, I don't feel quite well.' Now you know that's not like her. And then she stretched her arms and got a funny little smile. Didn't look sick at all, but her stomach *is* upset."

"She'll be all right," Friend Ed said quietly. "Women go through queer times." And he changed the subject. "One thing I've been meaning to ask you. Does Victor seem to hold a grudge for that bawling out you gave him?"

"Why, no. I don't think so. He's pretty quiet, doesn't talk much. Seems to go about his business and do his work. I think it did him good maybe."

"I was a little worried," said Friend Ed. "I thought maybe you shouldn't have hit him."

"I'm sorry about that," Joe Saul said. "I lost my temper. I told him I was sorry. I think he's forgot it."

"It wasn't like you to hit him or any man, Joe Saul."

"He said a thing. He said a thing that made me red mad. Do you hear Mordeen stirring around? I thought I heard her."

"I guess she's up," said Friend Ed. "I should be going. With all the work I've got to do on my place, I sit around in your kitchen after sun-up. Is your clock right?"

"Set it with the radio—it's always right."

A record started softly on the radio, a wailing torch song.

Joe Saul looked over at it. "I don't know how we managed before we had it. We hardly ever turn it off. It's like another person in the house. And Mordeen listens while she does the work." He sighed. "Let's have a fresh cup of coffee. Here, give me your cup. I'll wash it out."

He carried the cups to the sink and rinsed them.

The door opened and Mordeen came in. Her face was blooming and there was a small, satisfied smile on her mouth. She wore a quilted flowered dressing gown which reached almost to the floor.

Both men looked at her, and Joe Saul said, "Feeling better, Mordeen?"

"Oh, yes. Yes, much better."

Friend Ed said, "You look fine to me."

She moved to the couch under the window and sat down on it. "How beautiful a day," she said in wonder, as though it were the first day in the world.

"It's growing weather," Joe Saul said. "Shall I get you a little breakfast? There's oatmeal and crisp bacon in the warmer."

"You cook for me?" She laughed a low, happy laugh. "I should have got your breakfast. But it's nice to hear you offer, Joe Saul, it's very nice. No, I don't want breakfast."

"Coffee then? I'm just going to empty the pot and make a fresh one. Would you like some nice fresh coffee?"

"No," she said. "But I'm not really sick. I think I'm just indulging myself."

"It will be the first time," Joe Saul said. "It's a new thing with you."

She drew a deep breath, started to speak. "I—"

"Yes?" Joe Saul asked.

"I don't know what I started to say. My mind went flying off."

Joe Saul carried the filled cups of coffee to the table. "If you aren't going to have some, I won't make another pot, but maybe, if you don't feel well, I'd better. Victor will be in for his midmorning coffee soon."

Mordeen moved slowly in on what she had to say. She smiled to herself, and then her face was serious, and then she smiled again. She looked down at her hands, palm upward on her lap, one holding one, and the fingers relaxed and like a nest. "The doctor told me to take it very easy for a while," she said.

Joe Saul put down his cup and looked at her, twisting his chair around. "But he said you were all right. What does he think is the matter?"

And now she said it straight and clearly. "Joe Saul, I'm going to have a baby—*we're going to have a baby.*"

He did not hear at first because he had not been listening for it, but the words repeated themselves silently in his ears. His face set, looking at her, and the words repeated themselves again deep in his brain. For a moment Joe Saul fought his trembling chin. And then he put his head down on his arms and wept.

Friend Ed was looking at Mordeen, looking closely.

She looked back and her face was grave. She nodded. And then she smiled again.

An earthquake of emotion shook Joe Saul. Friend Ed looked away from him. But Mordeen smiled inwardly, watching her hands loving each other in her lap. Her face was withdrawn in mystery. The secrets of her body were in her eyes—the zygote new thing in the world, a new world but formed of remembered materials: the blastoderm, the wildly splitting cells, and folds and nodes, the semblance of a thing, projections to be arms and legs and vague rays of ganglia, gill slits on the forming head, projections to be fingers and two capacities from which to see one day, and then, a little man, whole formed, no bigger than the stub of a pencil and bathed in warm liquor, drawing food from the mother bank and growing. This frantic beingness lay under her loving hands embraced in a slow ecstasy in her lap.

And then Joe Saul stood up and walked heavily on his heels to the window and he looked out on his farm. He grasped his arms behind his back and pulled his shoulders up.

"Now," he said, "now it's all right." He raised his voice as though he called to the land. "Now it's all right." He laughed and turned his fierce delighted face back to the room. He released his arms and patted his hips gently as he spoke. "I've heard that in some parts of Europe they go out to the barns and tell the cattle. Why, every form is good and every ceremony." And he said, "Now that the black is lifted I can speak of blackness. So many of us nested in this land that we were it and it was part of us, so that the spring grass grew out of our pores and the green daggers of the corn came sprouting from our stomachs. You know, Friend Ed, how the unseasonable drought is like a dry-ness in the chest and how unplanned heat is a fever in us." He went on softly, "The generations of us—a totem, man on man, back to the first man—and the plans for future men and future great-grand men—all lying orderly in the blueprint chromosomes."

Friend Ed smiled. "I think you might like to give a party. I'll bring the twins. I'll get ice cream and whisky and I'll kill a turkey. This is a moment of great joy, Joe Saul. And where did I hear that?"

Joe Saul said, "Now that the black is up I can speak of black, but I can't remember it very well. I can't remember how it felt now the triumph is in me." He went to Friend Ed. "I see myself and myself's torment whirling away out of range of sight and feeling—torment in blood and heart that the line, a preciousness carried and shielded through the stormy millennia, is snapped, the product discontinued, the stamen mildewed."

"It's all over, Joe Saul. Would you like to invite some friends? Does Mordeen want it known so soon?"

They looked at her, and Friend Ed said more loudly to catch her attention, "Mordeen, do you want it known?"

She smiled. "Oh, yes. Why should I not? What is the matter, Joe Saul? Aren't you glad?"

"Glad? Oh, yes. But remembering—remembering the pain—it's like looking last in a coffin—there it is. The face is dead and you can forget it. But if you do not look, the face is never dead and you cannot in your back mind say good-by. And so I am looking back at the sadness so deep dug in. The top mind denies sterility. I remember how it was. Being convinced, I denied the desolation or made a joke of it—a bitter joke. I can remember only vaguely now the slow suspicious hatred that can grow and flower between man and woman while they say, 'Not now. We can't afford a child. We don't want a child if we can't take perfect care of it.' Or they say, 'We have great things to do in the world—great work that would be inhibited by a child. Our time is too precious for the squalling and noise and mess and—the expense.' "

"Would a party tire you, Mordeen?" Friend Ed asked. "Don't you think we should have a laughing party?"

"I do," she said. "I want a great scrabbling party full of noise, violent and crazy. That's what I want, Joe Saul. Come from your blackness now, Joe Saul."

"It's going fast," he said. "It's like a wound that, healing, leaves no memory, but only a scar of insensitive skin. Only the fecund can mention sterility at all. The sterile feel in their guts the desolate secret knife. Only the sterile really know through default the great two laws, that one must live and one must pass that life along—carry the fire and pass it down. The blood must flow, and the genes are ordered to communicate." He paused and shook his head violently.

Victor came up on the porch and entered the kitchen. He wore overalls and an open blue shirt. His arms were brown. "I thought I'd come in for a cup of coffee," he said. He caught some feeling from the room and was silent.

Joe Saul moved to Mordeen and looked at her as though she were new and unknown in his eyes. And she raised her head and her eyes brushed over Victor for a moment and then rose to face Joe Saul.

He said "Mordeen" softly, experimentally, as though he had never pronounced this name before. There was a wonder in his eyes. He sighed the great shuddering sigh that follows active love. He said, "Mordeen, we have a child," not telling her but tasting the words.

Victor's head snapped up. "What did you say?"

Then Joe Saul whirled on him. "You heard. We have a child," he shouted. "There's going to be a baby in this house. There's going to be a child playing in that dust. There's going to be a growing thing discovering the sky and kicking the chickens aside and finding eggs!" Joe Saul's body wove from side to side. He laughed hysterically in a surge of great joy. "There'll be great questions asked and answered. Do you understand that? We will rediscover the whole world. Can you hear that? This land will have its own plant growing out of it—born to it, knowing it."

His voice grew soft, almost whispered, and his eyes saw. "Our child will lie chest-flat, cheek-flat, against the ground. His toes will kick the dirt and his ear will listen and the earth will speak to him."

Victor smiled, a tight, concealing smile, and his eyes

met Joe Saul's and then passed on to Mordeen, and his smile deepened. "Congratulations, Joe Saul," he said. "This calls for celebration. But you say 'he.' How do you know it will be a boy?"

Joe Saul shouted, "How do I know? What do I care? I am not dead. My blood is not cut off. My immortality is preserved. I am not dead! Boy? Girl? There will be more—and boys or girls." He went close and pounded his fist gently on Victor's chest, forcing him back a little. "We have got a child," he said. "It's right there growing. It came from me—do you hear? It came from me. And it will be a piece of me, and more, of all I came from—the blood stream, the pattern of me, of us, like a shining filament of spider silk hanging down from the incredible ages."

Joe Saul sat down, exhausted. But in a moment he threw back his head and laughed.

Then Joe Saul rose up, prancing like a heavy horse, dancing unguilefully, and laughing too. He waltzed, his arms held out as though he balanced a partner; heavy footed he was, and his knees were bent. And the little radio played the waltz for him. And he was silly, as a joy-stuffed child is silly. Mordeen watched him, smiling, and Victor's eyes followed him, and Victor went disgustedly to fill the coffee pot. Friend Ed laughed at his antic clumsiness.

"I never have seen you this way, Joe Saul," he cried.

"I never had reason," said Joe Saul, and he stopped in his dancing.

"Well, reason or none, I have chores to do. They don't understand reasons—good or bad."

Joe Saul drew himself up in towering mock majesty.

"I here declare a holiday, a holy day," he orated. "I here declare that chores do not exist. Let your twins do them, or let them not be done. Argue with me, and I will flick my hand—like this—and your farm will disappear." He laughed at his own funniness. "Give me more argument, and I will flick twice—like this—and you will disappear." He whirled, "Victor, in the cabinet—get the whisky—get glasses. You want a party—it begins now. This empress"—he bowed toward Mordeen and, looking at her, his throat closed and the play went nearly out of him—"this queen, this mother wants a party. She has it. Hurry, Victor, before the party gets away," and Joe Saul ran to help to bring the glasses. He poured large portions.

Mordeen said, "None for me. I'd like it but I can't. I'll have to leave such things for a while."

In the middle of his gaiety Joe Saul became stone. He walked to the cot where she sat. He kneeled in front of her and put his hands on her knees. "Take care," he said. "Walk tenderly. Oh, take gentle care. Rest, and let your thoughts be high and beautiful." And he added hoarsely, "I order you to lift no burden, to encourage no weariness. You are to call me—me—when any work heavy or hard or long or even tiresome is to be done. Do you hear me? I order this."

She put her hand on his head affectionately and

moved her fingers in his hair. "I will obey you," she said. "And it's a pleasant thing. I will take care. But I'm not as delicate as you would think. There's a frightening endurance in expectant women. I will obey. Now have your drink." She put her hands under his elbows and raised him to his feet. "Drink! Begin your party."

His mood changed then. He stepped to the table and raised his glass. "To the Child!" he shouted, and he drained his glass, and Friend Ed and Victor drank after him.

Quickly he filled the glasses. And Friend Ed raised his glass high. "To the Mother," he cried.

They drank again. "That's good," Joe Saul said. "That's the one I should have said first. That's good, Friend Ed." He choked. "Ah! it's strong. I need a little water." He went to the sink and drew water and poured it down so quickly that the water ran from the corners of his mouth and dampened his blue shirt.

Victor was close to the table, passing the glasses. Victor's eyes burned with the quick impact of the whisky. A boldness was growing on him. He waited until Joe Saul came back to the table and then he raised his glass and looked at Mordeen.

"To the Father," he said.

Suddenly Joe Saul's eyes were wet. He drank his drink and slowly put down his glass. He went to Victor and put his arm around the broad young shoulders. "Thank you," he said. "Oh, thank you, Victor."

And Victor in triumph looked again at Mordeen. And he saw hatred in her face as he had never experienced—hatred so cold and dangerous that he could not counter it. His eyes wavered and fell and he turned away, and his eyes met Friend Ed's eyes, and there he saw an executioner looking at him with lethal, detached sternness, as though judging where to put the rope. He coughed and said loudly, "A few more toasts like that and I'd be drunk. I guess I'd better get to work." He went out of the kitchen and his footsteps hammered on the porch boards.

Joe Saul idly poured more whisky into the glasses. "I'm as skittish as a horse," he said, and he chuckled. "Strange, one moment I want to shout and I find myself weeping. I'm touchy as a range horse in the blowing papers of a picnic ground."

Mordeen stood up carefully. "If we're to have a party, I'd better rest," she said. "The excitement has tired me, tired me out."

"You should eat," Joe Saul said.

"No, not now. Later I'll drink some milk and eat a little toast."

"Lie down then. And if a party is too much, we'll have no party."

"Oh, I want a party—all the friends, the twins, the neighbors. But who's to cook and make the punch?"

"You go," Joe Saul said. "I'll get everything in town. I'll have it sent all ready. It would be a sad thing if I couldn't do this to celebrate our child."

She walked by him and her hand drew lovingly across his back.

Joe Saul watched her go and then he sat down and regarded his poured drink. "I'm tired," he said. "I'm suddenly very tired, as though the blood had poured out of me."

"It's akin to shock," Friend Ed said. "I guess it is a kind of shock. And now if you run true to form, you'll have morning nausea worse than hers, and when there is a little pain in her, your guts will twist in agony. And in labor—oh, God help you, Joe Saul, in labor!"

Joe Saul said, "I want to bring a present to her—some preciousness, some new beautiful thing to delight her, so that her eyes will dance, and she will say, 'Who could ever have thought that I would have a beauty thing like this.' "

"I think she has it."

Joe Saul stirred. "Yes, I know that. But something like a ceremony, something like a golden sacrament, some pearl like a prayer or a red flaring ruby of thanks. Some hard, tangible humility of mine that she can hold in the palm of her hand or wear dangling from a ribbon at her throat. That's a compulsion on me, Friend Ed. Come with me." He was excited again. "I must get this thing. My joy requires a symbol. Come with me to town. We'll get the partiness—all cooked and carved and poured. She's worked so hard before every party that only a little unweariness was left to enjoy it. I'll be the hands to do her work tonight. And then we'll look—I don't know what the beauty is—but I'll know it when I see it."

Now he had made up his mind he was excited again. "Hurry, Friend Ed. Drink your whisky and come with me. I don't feel trustful of myself to be alone." He walked to the door, and back to the door and back, like a terrier begging to be let out.

Friend Ed stood up slowly. He said satirically, "Be careful, Joe Saul. Remember the child. See you don't overdo. You must conserve your strength." And then he said seriously, "You don't want to be alone, but do you want Mordeen to be alone?"

"Ah!" Joe Saul said. "It's hard to remember. She has always been so complete and competent. Thank you for remembering. I'll call Victor, tell him to stay close. I'll take the old dinner bell to her. Then if she needs anything she can clang the bell and he will come."

Friend Ed said quietly, "I don't think Victor—" and then he knew that he could never say what he had thought.

"Victor's all right. Didn't you hear him? He's forgot I hit him in the face. Victor's a good boy." He opened the door and shouted "Victor!" and a far answer came. Joe Saul cupped his hands. "Victor, come here, I want to talk to you. Come on, Friend Ed." The two men went out and the door closed behind them. Alone on its shelf the little radio played on, the kettle bustled with steam. The ticking of the clock was very loud.

Now there were steps on the porch. Victor opened the door quietly and stood in the doorway, looking out, while an automobile engine roared and the sound whined up the gears and slowly rose to silence in the distance. Then Victor gently closed the door and walked lightly to the table. He poured himself a drink and drained the glass and quickly poured another. The neck of the bottle clashed against the tumbler. And through the open door to the bedroom Mordeen's voice called, "Is it you, Joe Saul?"

Victor sat quietly and sipped his drink, and his glance rose and remained on the door. He sat down in one of the straight chairs and leaned back, and the old chair creaked. Mordeen called anxiously, "Who's there?" And in a moment she stood in the doorway. She saw Victor and stopped and her hands went out and braced against the door frame. "Oh!" she said. "It's you. Why didn't you answer?"

Victor rocked his chair a little on its hind legs and he sipped the straight whisky in his glass. "Joe Saul asked me to take care of you while he's in town. He told me to, ordered me to."

"What do you want, Victor?" she asked in alarm. "You shouldn't be drinking now."

He finished the drink and idly poured another. His eyes felt over her body. "Come in," he said. "Come in and sit and talk to me."

For a moment she hesitated, and then her face became a mask, closed and wary and waiting. She crossed behind the table and sat down on the cot under the window. Outside a cow bawled mournfully for her calf.

Mordeen said woodenly, and softly, "What do you want, Victor?"

He swung his chair around, facing her. He rested his elbow on the table and he crossed his legs. "Just wanted to pass the time of day with you," he said. "I never seem to get to talk to you. Isn't that funny? I'd think you'd want to talk to me."

She stared at him, her eyes expressionless.

Victor tasted his drink and made himself more comfortable. His body slouched in his chair. The small gold medal shone at his throat. "And now I hear this interesting news, but not from you. I hear it from Old Joe Saul. It just seemed to me that you yourself would want to tell me all about it."

She said finally in a monotone, "When you finish your game, maybe you'll tell me what you want."

Victor smiled. "You don't want to pretend that you don't know what I'm talking about, do you?"

"I know what you're talking about," she said, "but I don't know what you are trying to say."

He uncrossed his legs and leaned toward her. "Do you think I have no interest in my child?" he asked.

She said without emphasis, "It's not your child, Victor. It's Joe Saul's child."

Now he laughed loudly. "Mordeen," he said, "do you think that if you say that often enough it will be true?"

"It is true," she said.

Now he leaped up angrily. "That's a lie," he cried. "You know it is and I know it is. You know Joe Saul can't have a child. You know that. I don't like being used. I don't like being shut out of something that's mine. Don't try tricks because I don't like them. This is my baby. I've got a lot of girls in trouble so I know *I'm* all right—but this is the first one that will be born. Don't you think I have some feeling for my own blood? Do you think I want to be used like a stud animal for the comfort of Joe Saul? Is that fair? He gets everything, and I get put back in the corral."

"You got what you said you wanted," she said coldly. "You got what you can understand."

"Don't do that again," he said angrily. "What I can understand and what I can't understand! I think I proved to you I could understand anything you can. Even if you wouldn't come near me again afterwards."

She said, "Victor, don't bother me."

"Don't bother you. First I don't understand and now don't bother you. I understand enough to be sure it's my child, and I'll bother you when you have my baby. Understand that!" He leaned toward her in rage, beating out his intention on the table with his closed fist.

His anger raised anger in her. She stood up and her voice fought against the control she put on it. "I told you, Victor, and asked and even begged you to believe that I would do anything in the world for Joe Saul's content because of my love for him."

"Yah!" he said snarlingly.

"I tell you again. I warn you to believe it."

"What's he going to say when he knows it's my baby, when he knows you were out in the barn with me when he was drunk?"

She cried fiercely, "It's Joe Saul's baby, conceived in love for him. I saw his face hovering over me. I felt his arms—not yours. You don't exist in this, Victor. The little seed may have been yours, I have forgotten. But no love was given or offered or taken. No! It's Joe Saul's baby. Joe Saul's and mine."

She glared at him like a mother cat, and her claws were out. And then she backed to the cot, her teeth bared and her nostrils flaring. She breathed in little bursts. "And no one, nothing will take that away. I had to do an alien thing, had to hide my hurt in a mountain cave of love to do it. You nor any consideration will take this child away from Joe Saul. Believe it, Victor. If I could do that thing before—think what I could do now."

Victor's body and his face were beaten by her force. He stood, walked toward the door. And suddenly he flung himself on the floor in front of her and embraced her ankles and laid his face down on her feet.

"Oh, God! I'm lonely." His despair was heavy as a gray stone. "What have I done, Mordeen? What crime have I committed? In the night I've thought of the things you said. Mordeen, I've laughed at them and I've run out to women to prove those words weren't true —and they are." He raised his face and looked at her.

"I wish I had never seen Joe Saul. I wish I had never seen your eyes on him hot and happy and shining. If I had not known, I could go to the town girls, fumble at their dresses, quiet their giggling and rut with them. But now I hear your voice over their little shrill squeals of pleased protest. I feel your strong sure warmth behind their chilly pimpled breasts." He said miserably, "I love you. And it's not like anything I have ever known. It is as different as—as—you said it once—as milk."

Her face had grown compassionate as she looked down at him. "Poor Victor, you will find it. If you are open to it, capable of returning it, this will come to you."

"I've argued this way, argued to myself, Mordeen. But I have found this kind of love, and it cries in my mind that it can't happen twice." He rose up to his knees. "It shouts to me that if I do not save this—this one I know beyond all doubt—I will lose my chance. Mordeen," he cried, "I'm frantic. I do not think I can live. I don't say this the way such things are said—I do not think I can live. I have a crazy animal clawing in my guts." And indeed he was doubled up with pain.

"Now you know," she said softly. "Now you know why I did what I did. I didn't think you were capable of knowing." In pity she put her hand on his forehead and smoothed his hair back. Outside, a thunderhead throttled the sun and the light in the kitchen grew dusky. The radio turned low intoned prices of wheat, barley, corn, oats, hay, hogs, steers, calves, sheep, in a murmured litany.

Mordeen said, "I guess a shower is coming. Can't you go away, Victor? If you feel so, wouldn't it be better if you were not here, because this pattern will not change? Nothing can change it. You've thought of killing Joe Saul, haven't you, Victor?"

"Yes," he said almost under his breath.

"That would not change it. I would still be Joe Saul's wife, and this one here would be his child. And you, Victor, would be colder than a lonely cold; you would die in the cold of hatred. Think carefully of going away. The year will turn, and it will be better and then better and then—gone in some best new thing."

The kitchen was quite dark now and a very far thunder rumble shook the air. Victor put his cheek down on her knees, and time and the year rolled over and over as the earth rolls, swaying like a tiring top. The year changed and the world swung through the great ellipse. The year and the season swung on about the house. In Mordeen the baby grew. And the year rolled on.

"I've thought of that too," Victor said. "I can say with my mind that I will go—but I would refuse it. That I know. For I think of the summer ending now and the stubble on the ground and the hay brushing the ridge pole in the barn and windfall apples on the

orchard earth. And you—a swelling below your breasts
and my child kicking against the soft wall, and turning,
and I not able to put my hand there and feel its moving
life."

"Hush, Victor. It is not your child. A year will
draw—is drawing—out your sorrow like a basting
thread."

"A year," he said in the darkened room. And thunder crashed distantly and a blue flickering flash shook
the room. "I know the passing year. The fall is chill-
ing down and the hoar frost does crisp and yellow
the strong grasses near the stream under the tattering
cottonwoods. The blackbirds flocked nervously a
week and now they are gone. The wind and the ar-
rowing wild ducks are driving to the south over the
burning sumac. And you—you walk heavily on your
heels, your shoulders back to balance the growing
weight of my child, and your face is glorious and your
eyes smile all day long and your mouth perhaps turns
upward, smiling in your sleep."

"Hush, Victor," she said wearily. "It's not your
child. And don't you think it is a little cold in here?
The rain will turn to sleet, I think."

The year slipped past, and the endless business of
the aging earth continued.

The wind whined a little ghost howl around the
corners of the house.

"A man can forget nearly anything in a year,
Victor."

"I know this year," he said miserably. "I know the

white drifts curving down to the silver ice in the shallows above the pond. I know the black lashing branches of the pear trees and the dogs snuffling and moaning in the storm porch. I can feel the ice-air burning in my nose and blue aching fingernails and the acid cider. They're bringing in a Christmas tree from the forest today. And you, Mordeen, quiet and tired with waiting—you move silently, with eyes and ears and touch turned inward to hear and see and feel my child."

She stirred in the steely light, moved heavily. "It's not your child. It's Joe Saul's child," she said with heavy monotony. "Turn on the light, Victor, and build up the fire. The cold is creeping in. The winter's really here. My year of bearing is nearly done. And very soon Friend Ed and Joe Saul will be coming with the Christmas tree. Shovel a wider path down to the road so they can get the tree in. They said it would touch the ceiling. And, Victor, I wish you could find the strength to go away. I've seen your suffering in this livelong year. But the birth will be soon now, Victor. Please try to go away. I have not changed my mind in the year. It's Joe Saul's child. I will protect him in this child. I threaten you, Victor."

He cried, "Mordeen, I love you. I cannot go away."

He stood up and turned on the light, opened the stove and poked the dying fire to flame. The light was nearly gone. The windows were edged with white and big feathered flakes were drifting down.

The steel winter lay on the land and crept to the

doors and windows and peered whitely in. And the snow put silence on the earth. Mordeen pushed herself heavily up from the couch. Her shoulders were back and the child was low and large in her body. She shuffled across the room, filled the teakettle, and put it on the stove. One of her hands stayed on her abdomen, as though to help support the weight which bore her down. Then she stood listening. "I think they're coming in. Go help them, Victor; help them get it through the door. And please remember what I said."

Victor looked out, and then he opened the porch door. A tumble of snow came in. Friend Ed and Joe Saul were sliding the fine fir tree butt forward up the path. They edged it up the stairs to the open door and Victor grabbed it and pulled the snowy branches through the door. Joe Saul and Friend Ed stood on the storm porch, stamping and beating their shoulders. They stood laughing there, taking off their coats and kicking the arctics from their feet, and then they came into the pleasant kitchen. Their cheeks were pink with cold and their eyes watered. They rubbed their hands together in the warmth.

"We'll have to cut it off," Friend Ed observed. "I told you it was too big."

Mordeen had brought a broom to sweep up the scattered snow before it melted. She moved slowly with a careful rolling step.

Joe Saul cried, "I'd rather have it too big and cut it off than too small and have to stretch it. Here, give me that broom, Mordeen. You shouldn't be doing that. Here, you sit down and let us do all this."

She smiled, saying, "It's been hard learning not to do my own work. You may regret you've made a sluggard of your wife."

"You'll learn to do it again." Joe Saul laughed. "But not now. The work you are doing is much more important. I was telling Friend Ed how startled I was when the baby moved—lying in bed, and I guess I was half asleep, and then I felt this little secret movement, and it wakened me." He looked upward, smiling in his remembering. "At first it was as though someone had touched me to catch my attention, but very gently. And then I felt a creeping like a soft cat—stealthy. And then there was a little push, and then—you can believe this or not—there was a shaking like silent laughter and then a scrabbling movement. I felt it climb up my spine and then come tumbling down again. And then the small shake of laughing. Well, it startled me. I thought at first one of the dogs had crawled in bed with us. And I sat up and turned on the light. Mordeen didn't even wake up. And do you know what it was?" He pointed. "It was that one playing in the darkness of his mother." He laughed with pleasure, and Mordeen smiled. Victor moved restlessly.

Friend Ed said, "I know how that is. And if you want to feel a real rumpus, you have twins sometime. I think they play volley ball. The doctor didn't say it's twins, did he, Mordeen?"

"No," she said, "it's only one. And it's turned and perfect. I saw it," she said in wonder. "I saw it on the X-ray plate. At first I didn't know what it was. Know what it looked like? Well, it looked like the nave of a cathedral with a vaulted roof and one great column—that was ribs and spine. At first I couldn't make out the child until Dr. Zorn showed me, and then, there he was, upside down and balled up like a kitten."

Joe Saul said excitedly, "What did he look like, what could you see?"

"Why, everything," she said. "His head and little arms and his legs and feet curled up. He's been a great jumper but now he's quiet. That worried me. I thought something might be wrong. But Dr. Zorn says he's just fine. He will be quiet now, the doctor says. He will sleep until he has to make the big fight."

Victor said nervously, "If you aren't going to set up the tree right now, I'd like to go out to my room. I don't feel clean."

"Go ahead," Joe Saul agreed. "We'll put up the tree after dinner." And Victor said, "I don't feel clean," and he almost ran from the room. Mordeen watched him go.

"I don't know how we'll get around that monster tree," Mordeen said. "It will nearly fill the room."

"And ought to," Joe Saul crowed. "Say, I'd like to see that picture. I wonder if I could get it."

"The doctor wants to study it," Mordeen said.

"But if you go to his office I'm sure he'll show it to you."

"Maybe afterwards he'll let me have it to keep," said Joe Saul. He sat down by the table and stretched his arms in luxury. "Next Christmas, Friend Ed, next tree we bring in—why, he'll be sitting under it. And he'll have his own presents. I wonder what I'll get him his first Christmas. I'll have to think about that. But I've got a whole year to think."

"Something round or soft or shiny the first year," Friend Ed advised. "That's about all that interests them the first year. Say, you'd better not call him 'him' all the time. It might be a girl."

"I don't care," Joe Saul said. "I'd like a girl. I'll like what I get." He turned to Mordeen. "You go in the bedroom and lie down and rest," he ordered. "I'm going to get dinner now. I'll call you when it's ready. Friend Ed is going to eat with us. He'll help me."

She stood up slowly and obediently. "I'm really spoiled," she said, smiling. "And I like it very well. You have a lazy wife, and it is your fault."

He stood up and went to her and took her face between his hands and looked in her eyes, holding her chin tilted up at him. And he chuckled with delight. "Look, only look, Friend Ed. Isn't she beautiful?" And suddenly his lips trembled and he looked away. And Mordeen moved heavily through the door.

Joe Saul stirred the fire and put a big pan on the heat. "It's going to be a fry supper," he said. "Whether

you like it or not, that's what you'll get, Friend Ed."
He moved quickly about at his preparation. "Fried liver
and stewed tomatoes and milk and tapioca for dessert.
Would you like a drink of whisky, Friend Ed?"

"I wouldn't mind."

Joe Saul brought bottle and glasses to the table and
poured two big drinks. "It will take a minute for the
pan to heat," he said. "Everything's ready. I did it all
this morning. When I fry the liver we can eat." He
drank half of his whisky and set the glass down on the
table. "It's strange, Friend Ed," he said. "Of course you
know the baby's there—of course it's there—but it's a
mystery. I suppose you don't quite believe it until it is
really born. But she has *seen* it, really seen the head and
arms and legs. That's different! That's a very different
thing. That makes it real. It's not just an idea any more
or a wish or a prayer. It's a real thing. Oh, I'll have to
see that picture! I'll have to see it. I'll go tomorrow."

"I see what you mean, Joe Saul. That's true."

The door burst open and Victor stood before them.
His eyes were wild. He was wrapped in an overcoat
and he carried a suitcase in his hand.

"I can't stand it. I'm getting out. I'm going—going
now—right now!"

Joe Saul looked at him in amazement. "Going?
What's wrong with you, Victor?"

"Well, I—I can't stand it, that's all."

"Can't you tell me what's the matter?" Joe Saul
asked.

A torturing struggle was taking place in Victor's

mind. His eyes were filled with fierce suffering, with hatred and longing and love.

Joe Saul asked, "Is it because I hit you in the face, Victor?"

For a moment Victor was still weighing, fighting with himself, and at last he chose his course. He looked at Joe Saul almost with compassion. "That's it," he said. "I can't stay in a place where I was hit in the face."

"But I apologized," said Joe Saul. "I said I was sorry. Did it hurt so much, Victor?"

"Yes, it did."

"I'm sorry. In a time of such joy, it seems a shame. Isn't there anything I can do?"

Victor fought himself, and his emotion overcame him. "No," he cried. "No. I'm going." He turned and ran as though he could not trust himself. He ran out of the door and left it standing open.

Joe Saul sighed. He went to the door and looked out and then he closed it gently and came back to the table. "I thought he had forgotten," he said. "I'm sorry he feels this way. He didn't even tell me where to send his pay."

Friend Ed spoke uneasily. "Let him go. He's young, and that's a brooding time, Joe Saul. That's a time when you inspect your hurts like little rocks. Let him go. There are many Victors. There will always be a Victor."

"I suppose you are right. I wish I had not hit him. I'm ashamed of that."

"Maybe he is ashamed too."

"Of what?"

"Of—running away."

"I'm sad because I was weak. I would not like to give weakness to my child."

He drank the rest of his whisky. "Remember, I said next year he'll have a present of his own. But he's a real thing now, with the picture. He's there and I can see him. He's closer than in another room. There's just a little soft wall between. Maybe he can hear and feel. I'm giving him a present soon."

"You're crazy, Joe Saul. You're just dog crazy."

"Maybe I am, but that's how I hope I stay. I had a strange thought. He's there, he's here. Why shouldn't he have a present this year? Why should he not?"

Friend Ed grinned. "Might be a little difficult to give to him. You're crazy, Joe Saul."

"Well, I could give him a present. I thought what I could give him. If I had the weakness to hit Victor, maybe I have others. I thought of it when I wanted to go in to Dr. Zorn to see the picture and now I think of it more. I want to give my son clean blood."

"You have," Friend Ed said uneasily. "What are you talking about."

"I want to give him the proof. That's what I mean—attested. I can get Zorn to go over me, head, heart, stomach, everything. Maybe I can say to this child—that's what your father gave you first of all— strength and health and cleanliness. That would not be a bad present, Friend Ed."

"I think you're really crazy," he said anxiously. "This is a silly thing. I don't like it. I don't want you to do it."

"*You* don't. Why don't you? I can give him the papers all signed by Dr. Zorn—maybe rolled like a parchment with a big seal and tied with a red ribbon like a diploma. I could hang it on the tree for him. His first present and the best."

"Don't do it. Zorn might think you're crazy, the way I do. He might put that in your paper."

But Joe Saul poured whisky in both glasses. He leaned across the table toward Friend Ed. "Don't tell Mordeen. I'll do it as a secret and as a kind of joke, but not a joke too. I haven't ever had a thorough check-up. It will please her, Friend Ed; don't tell her."

Friend Ed stood up. "I don't want you to do this. I don't like this. It's—it's crazy."

Joe Saul said quietly, "I think it is the sanest thing I have ever done. I don't know why I haven't done it before."

He raised his glass and cried, "I'm giving him a present. I must be sure it is perfect. I'm giving him the greatest present in the world. I'm giving my son *life*."

ACT THREE, SCENE I

The Sea

The tiny cabin of the little freighter was old and comfortable and well used. On one side stood a little mess table with a retaining ridge; good swivel chairs were bolted to the floor, and water bottles and glasses were placed in racks on a small sideboard. The walls were paneled in dark wood well oiled and rubbed for many years, and the brass brightwork shone. Against one wall, under hanging sea coats, was a broad chest upholstered as a bench. Two deep leather chairs stood in front of a small coal grate in a tile mantel, and on the mantel itself there was a model of a schooner complete and beautiful in its detail; beside it was a small artificial Christmas tree decorated with tinsel and silver and red glass balls. On the little hearth was a small rack of fire tools—a short heavy poker, a shovel, and tongs. On the wall under the portholes hung the trophies of many voyages to many places, assegai and knobkerries from Africa, war clubs and shark-toothed spears from the Polynesian south, daggers and stilettos, a witch mask or two, and a shrunken head, black and baleful, hanging by its hair.

The door stood open to the rail of the flying bridge and beyond—the night city of docks and behind them tall lighted buildings, and neon signs glowing in the sky.

A second closed door led to the sleeping cabins. A small coal fire glowed in the iron grate.

From outside came the sounds of the harbor, toot of tugs and mutter of engines, and steam hiss and rumble of deck winches and creak of lines in running gear. Behind the harbor sounds the city talked with streetcars and truck engines, with auto horns and juke-box music.

Mr. Victor in a blue mate's uniform and cap came into the cabin. He looked around nervously, then went to the little grate and stirred the coals, rattled the poker on the iron. A tug whistled a passing signal in the stream. And in the city a fire siren whined up the scale and down again. Mr. Victor stood looking at the little Christmas tree on the mantel. From the other side of the closed door Mordeen's voice came, muffled, calling, "Joe Saul!" Mr. Victor's head swung around. "Joe Saul!" the voice called with a note of alarm in it.

Mr. Victor went to the door and opened it. "He's not here," he said. "Come out, I want to talk to you." He went back to the grate and rubbed his hands close to the coals, and he said again toward the open door, "Come here, Mordeen. I want to talk to you."

In a moment she stood in the doorway, her hair disheveled from the pillow and her eyes wild and uncertain with sleep. She said, "I had a dream." And then as her mind came out of sleep, "Where did Joe Saul go?"

"He went ashore," said Mr. Victor. "He told me to stand by in case you needed anything."

"The time is close, Victor," she said. "I've had the

first ragged pains. Maybe false pains, but my time is close. I want Joe Saul here with me. I want him here." She walked back and forth in the heavy, rolling pace that restlessly precedes birth.

"Sit down," said Mr. Victor.

"No," she said. "I'm not comfortable sitting down." And then she laughed shortly. "A woman told me she always could tell when a child was due because she cleaned the bottom drawers of her bureau. Well, I just remembered the dust in the bottom of my cabinet, and I wanted to bend down, way down, to clean it out. I guess that's my sign. I want Joe Saul here. If he does not come back soon, I want you to look for him, Victor. It will be soon—oh, very soon."

A seething excitement filled Victor. He moved one of the big chairs a little. "No," he said at last, quietly but with a force controlled in his throat. "I can't! I tried, Mordeen. I tried to force myself. And I know that if it goes on a little more I will not—I will not know what I am doing." He held out his arms and he cried, "See, a chill is going on in me. My hands won't be quiet. Mordeen, I can't let you go."

"Let me go, Victor? What are you saying?" Her face was alarmed.

"I've given it every thought," he cried. "I can't do it. You are my woman and that is my child. I must have you."

"Are you crazy?" She stood in front of him. "I am not your woman!"

"Maybe crazy," he said. "And maybe I will get crazier. You must come away with me now. You are my woman and I cannot have my child born here."

"Mr. Victor," she said in command. "Go to your quarters. Go instantly. If Joe Saul heard you, he would have you off the ship or he would kill you. Go to your quarters!"

"No," he said, wondering. "It's too late. I must have you and my child." The hysterical intensity grew in his voice. "I must have that. It would be good if you wanted me as much as I want you, but I must have you whether you wish it or not. This is my whole life. I won't throw it away no matter what comes of it. Look!" he cried. "I tried to run away and leave you and my child to Old Joe Saul. And I couldn't do it. I came back. And I tried to be wise—to stand by like a cuckolded goat and see my woman and my child in Joe Saul's arms. *And I cannot do it.*"

"Victor," she said, "I've told you over and over why I need this child: I love Joe Saul. This is crazy."

"Crazy or not, that's the way it is," he said dully. "I will not lose the one life I have ever had—even if the world burns up."

She said kindly, "Poor Victor. You do not understand many things, and this you don't seem to understand at all."

"Maybe I don't have to understand," he said. "You are going away with me—now, tonight. I have a place for you. I have a doctor. You will come with me now.

You must come with me now"—his voice rose—"if I have to tear you free."

She was frightened at him now, sensing his growing hysteria. "I will not go, Victor. Don't you know that? Nothing can make me go. Don't you know that?"

His head was down and he shook it slowly from side to side. "There's only one other thing," he said. "We can wait here—just as we are. When Joe Saul comes I will tell him. I will tell him everything. I don't think you can look into his eyes and say, 'This is not true.' Then he will throw you out, and I will take you. In his rage he may hurt you—and the child. Is this worth doing, Mordeen? Or suppose he didn't—suppose he let it pass and you had to live with his covered hatred for you and his hatred for my child. I will surely tell him, Mordeen. Even if I don't want to, I will surely do it."

Her body bent over with pain. She leaned forward and her eyes distended and she bit her lips until the pain receded.

"It's starting. Give me time," she begged. "Please, Victor, give me time to think. I can't think now. Can't you see?"

"No," he said. "I've been over it too often in my mind. I don't dare give you time. No. I can't afford to give you time. It would cheat me," he shouted. "I tell you I don't dare. You must come away."

"I won't go," she said. "He will understand, and it will be all right."

"You don't believe that, Mordeen. If that were so, why didn't he adopt a child? Why his constant talk about blood and family? No, you don't believe that."

She came to him, pleading then. "Please, Victor, don't destroy three people for the sake of one. He has never hurt you. Why will you kill him, and through him me? What will you have then? Please, Victor. At least give me a little time."

"No," he said. "Time? Time is my enemy."

Suddenly she was calm and very tired. "Victor, many things have happened. With the child forming and growing in my womb, there is also a change in my mind. I am not the same as before. The hard self-corners are smoothed."

He asked uneasily, "Is this some trick?"

"No," she said quietly. "I don't think it is a trick unless it is a trick on me too. At first when I asked your help I was closed off in a little house of pain. There were no others in my world except Joe Saul and me. But in the long heavy months my world has grown. It is not closed off."

Victor said restlessly, "What are you trying to do?"

"I'm trying to tell you that you could be welcome now."

"How about Joe Saul?" he demanded.

"That has not changed. I love Joe Saul. I will not have him hurt. I am his wife."

"What kind of a fool do you think I am? Are you saying you would love both of us?" he demanded.

"Not in the way you mean, Victor. But I would try to open the family like a garment and take you in."

"Do you think you could be wife to two men?"

"No, Victor. I can be wife only to Joe Saul."

"Then I say no," he cried. "No!"

She looked at him closely then to make sure he would not change. "Please, Victor."

"No."

"Victor," she cried, "you don't know what your choice means! You don't know me. Please, Victor. You don't know. Why should you throw your life away? Don't do it, Victor! I beg you not to do it."

He said dully, "I've thought about it long, Mordeen. Lying in my bunk, hearing you laughing and planning with Joe Saul—how do you think that feels? Mordeen, if my choice were made with the certainty that I would die tomorrow, I would still make it. You must come away."

"You're sure, Victor? Can't there be some change? Can't you give me—at least a little time? Please, Victor—time."

"No," he said. "I can't go back now. I'm in a long narrow tunnel and I can't turn."

For a long moment she looked at him, and her eyes were full of tears. Neither of them saw Friend Ed standing in the doorway, looking in at them. His dark blue captain's uniform concealed his figure in the half-darkness.

Mordeen shook her head slowly. "I don't have a choice?" she said.

"No, you don't have a choice. Get a coat. That's all you are to take. Everything will be new—everything."

She sighed deeply. "Don't you know I will kill you, Victor?"

"Hurry," he said. "Only a coat. I don't want anything more from this old life."

She looked at him quietly, and her eyes set with resolve. She moved to the rack of coats and lifted down a long gray cloak.

"Victor," she said, "will you get the suitcase under my bunk?"

"What suitcase?" he demanded suspiciously. "I don't want anything from this life."

She turned toward him. "It's for the hospital," she said. "I've had it packed for weeks."

He hesitated.

"Get it, Victor," she said.

He went to the door, and as he passed through she hurried to the relics on the wall and drew a short thick knife from its sheath and concealed it in the folds of her cloak. And as she did, she saw Friend Ed standing just inside the door, shaking his head slowly at her. She stood perfectly still, her mouth open a little.

Victor came from the sleeping cabin carrying the suitcase. He saw Friend Ed. He dropped the suitcase on the floor and moved quickly toward him.

"What the hell do you want?" he demanded.

But Friend Ed looked past him at Mordeen. "Once I wouldn't help you," he said. "I wouldn't take the responsibility. Now I will."

"Get out of here!" Victor said.

"Hush," said Friend Ed.

Mordeen said, "I did it all myself. I don't need your help."

"But you have it now," Friend Ed said. "Whether you want it or not, you have it."

"Stay clear!" she shouted at him. "Stay clear of this! What I have started I will finish."

"I have my sailing orders," he said. "I sail at midnight. I came to say good-by." He looked at Victor. "Will you come on deck with me?" he asked. "I have a message for you."

"Say it here," Victor said harshly.

"No, it's a secret. Come!" He gently urged Victor through the door, and the two disappeared into the night.

Mordeen stood rigid, her eyes wide with fright. She waited for what she expected—then came the crunching blow, the expelled moaning cry, and in a moment the little splash. She shivered.

She was still staring straight ahead when Friend Ed came in again. He walked over to her and gently took the knife from her and replaced it in its sheath. He came back to her and took her arm and helped her to a chair and seated her.

He said, "Where's Joe Saul? I came to say good-by."

She roused herself from shock. "He was not bad, Friend Ed. He was not evil."

"I know," he said.

"I can't think," she said. "It's coming—the pains are coming."

Joe Saul stood in the open door, his legs apart, his shoulders down; his chin was hard with rage and his eyes flared with fury. Mordeen moved toward him. Then she saw his hard eyes that looked through and past her, and she moved timidly to the chest under the hanging coats, as though to hide.

Friend Ed cried, "I've been looking for you. I've got my orders. I'm sailing at midnight. What's the matter with you, Joe Saul? Have you been drinking?"

"Drinking? No!" he cried in rage. "I'm a sick man. That's what. I'm—sick!"

Friend Ed spoke in despair. "You went to Dr. Zorn!"

"Yes, I went. I went. I went all by myself. No one asked me to go. Goddamit, no one asked me to go!"

Friend Ed said hopelessly, "You went to Dr. Zorn. You know!"

Mordeen embraced herself in silent agony.

Joe Saul's eyes became wary. He did not meet Friend Ed's eyes. He did not look at Mordeen. "It's my heart. Doc Zorn says I have a bad heart. Me—a bad heart. I was sick once when I was a boy. That caused it."

Friend Ed spoke to Joe Saul as though he were a child. "Well, is it dangerous?"

Joe Saul cried, "Dangerous! He says I'll have to take it easy. Take it easy—me!"

Friend Ed sat in a swivel chair at the end of the

table and laughed and laughed. "What's wrong with that? Might be a good thing to take it easy. I'd like to myself. Give you more time with the baby."

Joe Saul said venomously, "I guess so. Mr. Victor has read all the books—now he can do some work."

Mordeen covered her face with her hands.

Friend Ed said, "Forget Victor. Victor is not here."

But Joe Saul went on, unhearing. "Someday he'll be master of a big liner, ladies and the captain's dinner, and he'll go up to the bridge once every watch just to see that everything's all right—but the sea's not in him. It will be a big hotel floating back and forth—maybe so big that they don't even turn it around—like a ferry boat."

"Stop it," Friend Ed said. "Don't blame Victor."

And Joe Saul said harshly, "At the bleak opening of the world we edged along the points in burned-out logs, feeling the coasts. We were sailors. Then with rush sails on cross-tied sticks we moved over the waters, and we raised a little light on the world so that it was not edged in darkness. We shipped long sweeps to beat against the winds and currents. We ranged up the coasts, up and down, from Sidon to Cornwall, from Carthage to Good Hope. And then—oh, timidly we put out into the blackness, crept blindly out and found it was not black at all but another bright world. We knew by roll and creak, by smell and the patterned flight of birds, by brown mud in the sea or floating weeds or a tormented school of herring how it was with the world and with the weather."

Friend Ed said quickly, "Be sure you aren't lying, Joe Saul."

But Joe Saul went on bitterly, "Mr. Victor's all right, and if he's not sure he has a book. But he does not see without looking nor hear without listening. When we came in the harbor he nearly ran down a scow because his hand did not swing over. He had to think and we nearly cut the scow in two. But I was there. Maybe now I will not be there. Maybe another time I'll be in my bunk, a sick man, and on the bridge—Mr. Victor. And I'm the one who wanted to give a present—a present of perfection—a Christmas present."

Friend Ed stood up and walked to the grate and warmed his hands for a moment while he thought. He moved the glowing coals with the short poker. And suddenly he made his decision. He touched Mordeen on the shoulder and strode back to stand over Joe Saul. "You're lying to me, Joe Saul. I don't remember any time before when you had to lie to me. And I would let you lie and gradually come out with your nasty truth, but there's no time. I'm sailing at midnight. So drop your lie."

Joe Saul asked, "What lie?"

"You know what lie. Your heart. That's not it, Joe Saul, and you know it. After all this time you've dug up your hard icy fact and finally you've got to face it. And if I'm to help you as my right and duty say, then I've got to help you with the truth. Name it, Joe Saul, name it, goddam you!"

Joe Saul shivered and his body shrank and he sat down heavily in one of the swivel chairs. His mouth worked helplessly. He said, "I forced it. Zorn didn't want me to see. I forced him. I made him let me see. I was crazy with power and joyfulness. I told him I would go to another man if he did not let me see. I made him let me look in the microscope."

Mordeen stood up and gripped the mantel with her hands. Friend Ed glanced at her and then moved a little to cover the sight of her from Joe Saul. Friend Ed said, "For a fool a happy lie is good enough. But I had hoped you were a little wiser. If you were wiser, the truth could be a glory for you."

Joe Saul went on, "I made him let me look. I saw the slide—big as a porthole it looked, and blinding with light. I turned the knob, and there they were. I saw them—shrunken and crooked and dead, corpses of sperm—dead. And, oh, my God!" Joe Saul covered his eyes with his hands.

Friend Ed got up and stood over his friend in pity. He tried to think. "I haven't much time," he said. "What can I do for you, Joe Saul?"

Joe Saul spoke behind his hands. "What can anyone do? It is finished. My line, my blood, all the procession of the ages is dead. And I am only waiting a little while and then I die."

Friend Ed sighed. He looked to Mordeen for help and then he chose his hard course.

"What are you going to do, Joe Saul?" he said

harshly. "Take down your hands. Stop trying to hide in the dark behind your fingers. The world still goes on outside. What are you going to do? What are you going to think? I haven't got much time."

Joe Saul raised his head. "I haven't had much time to think," he said.

"You've had all your life to think. You haven't dared."

Now rage came flooding up in Joe Saul's body and in his mind. "I'll have to kill him," he said hoarsely. "There is no place in the whole world for him to live, knowing and sneering, maybe never telling but always knowing. I cannot have his mind living in the same world with me."

Friend Ed said, "Forget Victor, forget Victor. How about Mordeen?"

Joe Saul bared his teeth and looked at the wall in front of him. "I can't get my mind open to her treachery. I feel that if I let myself look at her or think even for a second about her that I'll go down in a horrible pit with my hands on her throat. Stop torturing me, Friend Ed! Stop torturing me!" And Joe Saul covered his eyes again and his body shook. "There's no place for me to live in the whole world," he said.

Mordeen crept to the chair and hid in it.

Friend Ed's voice cut into Joe Saul like a wet rawhide thong. "Stand up, you cowardly, dirty thing! Stand up, or by Christ I'll hit you sitting down! Stand up!"

Joe Saul looked up in wonder at this rage. He came slowly to his feet. "What's this, Friend Ed?"

"Friend nothing. So much I can take and no more. What is this crawling, whining ego of yours that's so important? How can you dare out of your silly self to crush a lovely thing? Have I wasted my life being friend to a whimpering nastiness?"

"Friend Ed, what are you saying? Don't you understand?"

"I do understand. I understand that you are offered a loveliness and you vomit on it, that you have the gift of love given you such as few men have ever known and you throw on it the acid of your pride, your ugly twisted sense of importance."

"Friend Ed, Friend Ed, don't you understand? It's not my child, it can't be."

"It *is* your child. More than you can conceive in your sick soul. Soul? I wonder what your soul looks like. I think I know—it looks like those dead shrunken sperm." Friend Ed's voice spat at him so that Joe Saul raised his hands as though to protect himself from blows.

"She is giving you a child—yours—to be your own. Her love for you is so great that she could do a thing that was strange and foul to her and yet not be dirtied by it. She ringed herself with love and beauty to give you love and beauty. How wrong she must have been to love a fool—and a filthy fool."

"But why couldn't she tell me? Why did I have to discover—"

"Because you couldn't receive it. Because in your smallness you had not the graciousness to receive this gift. You cannot live because you have not ever looked at life. You crush loveliness on the rocks of your stinking pride. I wonder if you ever could understand." Friend Ed stood towering over Joe Saul and suddenly, without warning, struck him in the face with his open hand, struck him with complete contempt.

Joe Saul's eyes were wide. His hand rose slowly and touched his reddening cheek. And he looked at his fingers. His body sank slowly into the chair, but his eyes, wide with wonder and confusion and pain, did not leave Friend Ed's face.

And Friend Ed's mouth trembled and his eyes were sad. He kneeled down beside the chair and put his arm around Joe Saul's shoulders. "I've given you everything a friend can give, Joe Saul—even contempt, and that's the hardest thing of all. Killing is easy compared to that." And he said, "You didn't hear what I had to say. I'm sailing at midnight. I've done everything I can—everything. Now you will be all alone on your particular dark ocean. Maybe your soul will require the destruction of everything beautiful around it for its small integrity. But I always thought it might be a little braver soul than that, Joe Saul. It is so easy a thing to give—only great men have the courage and courtesy and, yes, the generosity to receive."

Joe Saul looked blankly away from Friend Ed and closed his eyes.

Friend Ed went on, "Now you are alone. I don't

know what you will do or think. But I can't believe, I can't think, that all my life I have been a friend to meanness."

Joe Saul's eyes wandered away and then came back. "Don't leave me, Friend Ed! For God's sake, don't leave me alone! I'm afraid. I don't know what to do." His voice was pleading. "Don't leave me alone."

Friend Ed spoke softly. "I told you—I have my sailing orders. I have to go."

"I'm afraid. I don't know what to do."

"I don't know what you'll do, Joe Saul. But I would hope that some greatness might be left in you. They say that crippled men have compensations which make them stronger than the strong. I could wish that you would know and understand that you are the husband and the father of love. The gift you have received is beyond the furthest hope of most men. It's not that you should try to excuse or explain. You should—you must—search in your dark crippled self for the goodness and the generosity to receive."

Joe Saul looked at him in wonder. "Are you sure that this is true, Friend Ed?"

"I am sure—oh, I am sure. But you—if you ever require sureness you have a long twilight way to go."

Joe Saul said, "It's a new, an unknown road. I don't know that I can find it alone."

"You'll never find it any other way. Come say good-by to me, Joe Saul. Say a good wish to me standing off to sea, and to yourself—standing off. Come, Joe Saul. Take the first steps. Come, Joe Saul." His hand put a little pressure behind Joe Saul's shoulders and almost forced him to his feet. Friend Ed took Joe Saul's cap from the table and put it on his head and straightened it. And he buttoned the two top gold buttons of Joe Saul's uniform.

Joe Saul said brokenly, "Friend Ed—"

"Hush. You'll have to work it out. You'll have to work it out—alone."

He pushed Joe Saul out and stood with him against the rail. And then Friend Ed came back and stood in the doorway looking into Mordeen's eyes. And he bowed with respect and love. Then he went quickly away. Joe Saul stood gazing after him.

Mordeen got up and moved toward the door, and then a great convulsion shook her and beat her down, and another struck her to her knees. She struggled and writhed on the floor and at last she screamed hoarsely in labor.

Joe Saul rushed in. "Mordeen," he cried. He saw her twisting on the floor. He ran to her and gathered her against his breast. He raised his head and shouted, "Mr. Victor! Mr. Victor, hurry, goddam you! Victor, come help me!"

ACT THREE, SCENE II

The Child

The small square room was white, impersonal, undecorated, a cell, a little sterile box with a wide door on one side. And in its center stood a high hospital bed and bedside table with a glass of water and a glass straw. And the room was muffled and silent, secret and cut off from every world.

Mordeen lay in the bed, her hair spread over the pillow, and a bundle, silent and covered, was beside her. Her face was masked with gauze and she lay very still, but her breathing was hoarse and her chest rose fiercely, struggling to bring a rush of pure air to her lungs. Then slowly her head turned from side to side and she muttered and moaned, fighting her way up from drugged unconsciousness.

The wide swing door opened and he stood in the entrance. He wore cap and long white tunic. The face, except for the eyes, was covered with a surgical mask. He came softly around the bed and looked down at her under the soft night light. And then he looked down at the muffled bundle that lay beside her. And his gloved hand gently pulled the covering aside.

"Mordeen!" he said softly.

As though she heard him, she took a great gasp of

air into her lungs and her head twisted from side to side. "Dead," she whispered. "Dead—the whole world—dead—Victor dead."

He said, "No, Mordeen, not dead—here and alive, always."

She threshed her head violently and she whimpered, "Friend Ed, I wanted—I wanted him to have his child. I wanted—but it's dead. Everything is dead."

Joe Saul said, "Listen to me, Mordeen. He is here —and resting. He's had great effort and now he's sleeping—a little wrinkled and very tired—and the soft hair—" He looked down. "And his mouth—the sweet mouth—like your mouth, Mordeen."

Her eyes snapped open and she struggled up. "Joe Saul, where are you? Joe Saul? Why did you go? Where did you go?"

He pressed her back against the pillow and took a cloth from the table and dried her wet forehead.

"I'm here, Mordeen. I didn't go away, or, if I did, I came back. I'm here."

And she muttered, "Who is dead? Is Joe Saul dead?"

"I'm here," he said. "I went away into an insanity but now I'm back."

"Maybe he'll never know," she said secretly. "Maybe he'll never guess. Maybe Joe Saul will be content." Her chest constricted and she held her breath.

He wiped her forehead until her throat relaxed. "Rest," he said. "I do know and I know more. I know that what seemed the whole tight pattern is not important. Mordeen, I thought, I felt, I knew that my particular seed had importance over other seed. I thought that was what I had to give. It is not so. I know it now."

She said, "You are Joe Saul? Faceless—only a voice and a white facelessness."

"I thought my blood must survive—my line—but it's not so. My knowledge, yes—the long knowledge remembered, repeated, the pride, yes, the pride and warmth, Mordeen, warmth and companionship and love so that the loneliness we wear like icy clothes is not always there. These I can give."

"Where is your face?" she asked. "What's happened to your face, Joe Saul?"

"It's not important. Just a face. The eyes, the nose, the shape of chin—I thought they were worth preserving because they were mine. It is not so.

"It is the race, the species that must go staggering on. Mordeen, our ugly little species, weak and ugly, torn with insanities, violent and quarrelsome, sensing evil—the only species that knows evil and practices it —the only one that senses cleanness and is dirty, that knows about cruelty and is unbearably cruel."

She tried to sit up, tried to raise herself. "Joe Saul, the baby was born dead."

"The baby is alive," he said. "This is the only important thing. Be still, Mordeen. Lie quietly and rest. I've walked into some kind of hell and out. The spark continues—a new human—only being of its kind anywhere—that has struggled without strength when every force of tooth and claw, of storm and cold, of lightning and germ was against it—struggled and survived, survived even the self-murdering instinct."

"Where is he?" she asked.

"Look down. Here he lies sleeping, to teach me. Our dear race, born without courage but very brave, born with a flickering intelligence and yet with beauty in its hands. What animal has made beauty, created it, save only we? With all our horrors and our faults, somewhere in us there is a shining. This is the most important of all facts. *There is a shining.*"

Her eyes were clearing now and her brain climbed up out of the gray ether cloud. "You are Joe Saul," she said. "You are my husband—and you know?"

"I know," he said. "I had to walk into the black to know—to know that every man is father to all children and every child must have all men as father. This is not a little piece of private property, registered and fenced and separated. Mordeen! This is *the Child*."

Mordeen said, "It is very dark. Turn up the light. Let me have light. I cannot see your face."

"Light," he said. "You want light? I will give you light." He tore the mask from his face, and his face was shining and his eyes were shining. "Mordeen," he said, "I love the child." His voice swelled and he spoke loudly. "Mordeen, I love our child." And he raised his head and cried in triumph, "Mordeen, *I love my son*."

FOR THE BEST IN PAPERBACKS, LOOK FOR THE

In every corner of the world, on every subject under the sun, Penguin represents quality and variety—the very best in publishing today.

For complete information about books available from Penguin—including Penguin Classics, Penguin Compass, and Puffins—and how to order them, write to us at the appropriate address below. Please note that for copyright reasons the selection of books varies from country to country.

In the United States: Please write to *Penguin Group (USA), P.O. Box 12289 Dept. B, Newark, New Jersey 07101-5289* or call 1-800-788-6262.

In the United Kingdom: Please write to *Dept. EP, Penguin Books Ltd, Bath Road, Harmondsworth, West Drayton, Middlesex UB7 0DA.*

In Canada: Please write to *Penguin Books Canada Ltd, 90 Eglinton Avenue East, Suite 700, Toronto, Ontario M4P 2Y3.*

In Australia: Please write to *Penguin Books Australia Ltd, P.O. Box 257, Ringwood, Victoria 3134.*

In New Zealand: Please write to *Penguin Books (NZ) Ltd, Private Bag 102902, North Shore Mail Centre, Auckland 10.*

In India: Please write to *Penguin Books India Pvt Ltd, 11 Panchsheel Shopping Centre, Panchsheel Park, New Delhi 110 017.*

In the Netherlands: Please write to *Penguin Books Netherlands bv, Postbus 3507, NL-1001 AH Amsterdam.*

In Germany: Please write to *Penguin Books Deutschland GmbH, Metzlerstrasse 26, 60594 Frankfurt am Main.*

In Spain: Please write to *Penguin Books S. A., Bravo Murillo 19, 1° B, 28015 Madrid.*

In Italy: Please write to *Penguin Italia s.r.l., Via Benedetto Croce 2, 20094 Corsico, Milano.*

In France: Please write to *Penguin France, Le Carré Wilson, 62 rue Benjamin Baillaud, 31500 Toulouse.*

In Japan: Please write to *Penguin Books Japan Ltd, Kaneko Building, 2-3-25 Koraku, Bunkyo-Ku, Tokyo 112.*

In South Africa: Please write to *Penguin Books South Africa (Pty) Ltd, Private Bag X14, Parkview, 2122 Johannesburg.*